JOHANNE, JOHANNE . . .

Lars Sidenius

JOHANNE, JOHANNE . . .

Translated from the Danish by Paul Larkin

DALKEY ARCHIVE PRESS

Originally published as *Johanne, Johanne . . .* in 2012 by Forlaget Fahrenheit.

Library of Congress Cataloging-in-Publication Data

Names: Sidenius, Lars, 1949- author. | Larkin, Paul, translator.
Title: Johanne, Johanne . . . / Lars Sidenius ; Translated by Paul Larkin.
Other titles: Johanne, Johanne. English
Description: 1st ed. : Victoria, TX : Dalkey Archive Press, 2016.
Identifiers: LCCN 2016006315 | ISBN 9781628971323 (pbk. : alk. paper)
Subjects: LCSH: Young women--Fiction. | Sexting--Fiction. | LCGFT: Cell phone
   novels.
Classification: LCC PT8177.29.I85 J613 2016 | DDC 839.813/8--dc23
LC record available at http://lccn.loc.gov/2016006315

This book was partially funded by the Illinois Arts Council, a state agency.

  Ireland Literature Exchange
Idirmhalartán Litríocht Éireann

The publisher acknowledges the financial assistance of Ireland Literature Exchange (translation fund), Dublin, Ireland.

Dalkey Archive Press publications are, in part, made possible through the support of the University of Houston-Victoria and its program in creative writing, publishing, and translation.

Dalkey Archive Press
Victoria, TX / McLean, IL / Dublin

www.dalkeyarchive.com

Cover: Art by Eric Longfellow

Printed on permanent/durable acid-free paper

From that moment onwards, her life was
a tangled web of lies, with which she
veiled her love in order to conceal it.
FLAUBERT, *MADAME BOVARY*

OCTOBER

15. Oct. 18.52

Hey there Jonah came across ur business card and just thought Id say hello. x johanne.

. . .

18. Oct. 11.30

Yeah that was a mare of week at work – finally caught up on my beauty sleep now tho! x johanne

. . .

22. Oct. 13.41

Why dont we meet up sometime?

. . .

26. Oct. 11.52

If I came over 2 ur office with a letter or something, will u invite me for a cup of coffee or tea? maybe later 2day or some other time this week?

26. Oct. 14.05

Enjoy the trip 2 the sunny south, u lucky thing. hope its worth it. really looking 4ward 2 coffee on friday.

. . .

29. Oct. 10.11

Hope uve landed safe and sound :) c u soon!

29. Oct. 19.25

Thnx 4 coffee – really enjoyed it :) we must do that
again!?

. . .

30. Oct. 13.05

Gr8 u got madame bovary. enjoy!

. . .

31. Oct. 17.26

I read a bit of Macunaima after u praised it so much. like
I said. I didnt really know Andrade before this, but really
interesting 2 read a bit of early magic realism – very
sensual :)

NOVEMBER

3. Nov. 11.20

Yeah were super busy in lead up 2 the bookfair, but I spose its same 4 u all?

. . .

4. Nov. 20.39

Oh yes! Lærke loves her cup cakes, but try getting her 2 eat her dinner after she's been 2 a cafe ffs.

4. Nov. 20.55

Shes very headstrong. wonder where she got that from? :)

. . .

10. Nov. 15.26

Just wanted 2 hear about ur staff meal tomorrow evening. Im going 2 b there with someone else from here. do u know if theres a lot going 2 it?

10. Nov. 15.58

Sounds gr8! hope we get the chance 2 chat, just as professionals of course, no need 2 mention our coffee tet a tets :)

. . .

12. Nov. 13.35
Thnx 2 u all 4 the meal last night Jonah. nice 2 meet everyone and lets hope something comes of it in terms of the proposed collaboration.

. . .

14. Nov. 21.36
Think I went past the entrance 2 ur apartment block 2day. Lærke plays with a kid in ur area. phew. feel the real single mother sometimes.

. . .

14. Nov. 21.50
That's allrite for u 2 say, but it can b hard 2 have a career and b a full on mother at the same time :)

. . .

15. Nov. 11.03
Yes Im well aware it was me chose 2 have a kid – but maybe I was a bit 2 young 2 make that choice.

15. Nov. 11.36
Yes I know that 2, but ur son is nearly an adult and lives with his girlfriend.

. . .

16. Nov. 19.05

Japanese tea sounds lovely, probably best if I come over
2 u – in about half an hour?

. . .

17. Nov. 11.45

Hey u! not quite myself 2day, wasn't easy 2 leave ur bed.
it was incredibly warm and soft. I can come back 2 it
later 2day if u want? I can get a sitter for Lærke.

. . .

18. Nov. 11.26

Just wanted 2 make sure u got that being in ur bed is
fucking fantastic!

. . .

19. Nov. 01.37

My tipsy doppelganger and I were on the verge of
invading ur flat on the way home from that party, but we
were good girls – didnt want 2 disturb ur sweet dreams
hon :)

. . .

20. Nov. 11.40

I should have turned right round and gone back 2 u that instant. kissed u and dragged u into that bed again.

20. Nov. 12.49

I'm fairly certain I could spend the whole weekend just lying in ur bed making love. Gustav mustnt find out of course. maybe he doesnt give a shit anyway – he never asks and has never shown any real interest in me 4 like centuries? But u know that anyway.

. . .

21. Nov. 18.30

I also have loads of time on my hands in the coming week. Gustav has left town. fortunately he took Lærke with him. I know the whole things not exactly straight4ward, but it would be really grrrrr8 if you were keen 2 see me all the same.

22. Nov. 00.14

Right then. c u wednesday. sweet dreams :)

. . .

22. Nov. 16.17

No why do you think ur off my radar? :) things just crazy busy all of a sudden. 2 Swedish crime stories that r really taking off.

22. Nov. 16.30

As we speak there's something weird going on in my body and Im seriously wondering whether I shud run down and buy the morning after pill b4 its too late. no joking!

22. Nov. 17.05

Actually I dont think it matters that much right now. if its happened its happened but we'll assume all is OK :)

. . .

23. Nov. 10.07

Morning. thought Id let u know 2morrow evening seems 2 long 2 wait right this second.

. . .

24. Nov. 12.05

Sooooooo much want 2 b stark naked with u the whole evening and night. fantasizing we are already.

24. Nov. 15.09

Holy shit! U got my aching loins all a shiver. not long now!!

. . .

25. Nov. 11.39

My thoughts cant keep away from those wonderful orgasms u gave me yesterday. Im still getting aftershocks over my whole body – have 2 try and focus on something else now ffs. Ive never felt this way b4.

25. Nov. 14.59

I really hope u managed 2 wash ur face properly b4 that seminar :) u had me gushing wet yesterday.

25. Nov. 15.07

Im fairly sure I drenched most of ur bed, ur sofa and table as well.

25. Nov. 22.36

U guys obviously have an extensive programme 2 get thru there. Ive just been discussing pubic hair shave not shave with my workmate petra whos a lesbian, think u know her :) Id really love 2 go home right how. but cant leave till later. when r u finished?

26. Nov. 00.04

U can b a bit annoying sometimes! hope I can get away soon. have an urgent need 4 ur bed.

26. Nov. 01.11

nite nite hon :)

. . .

26. Nov. 11.22

Oops that was supposed 2 b annoying with a smiley
after it :) in a brilliant mood myself. quiet day here at the
office. and u?

26. Nov. 11.39

Ok. r u all going out 2 eat as well? were going 2 Cofoco
– pickled vegetables and lovage mayo, yum.

26. Nov. 11.42

Yeah, sure can. if thats OK with you?

26. Nov. 12.03

Oh yes :)

26. Nov. 12.54

Im coming!

. . .

27. Nov. 12.14

Stabbing pains in the heart? Dont like the sound of that,
Im sure the doctor can sort that out. Hope u slept well
and that u still want 2 c me tomorrow. even tho I dont
know that much about men and am not one for head
over heels stuff.

27. Nov. 13.10

Too flighty. no – thats not my style of humor at all . . . 2
flighty – hello!?

27. Nov. 14.52

:) no, ur reading me totally wrong. really looking forward
2 seeing u. then u have 2 decide whether u can spank
and discipline me 2 my senses, or whether Im just a
totally hopeless project.

27. Nov. 15.08

Thnx. I will seriously consider signing up as a private
pupil in ur school for instruction in the opposite sex –
the laying on of hands and magic energy field massage
sounds like my kind of class :)

27. Nov. 17.42

My shallow knowledge of the opposite sex? – that's not
funny at all. 2 b honest I think uve managed 2 shake my
self confidence so much I dont think we can see each
other tomorrow . . .

27. Nov. 18.50

Er . . how did we let things go so far? you know fine well
I really want 2 spend time with u. but sometimes u make
me feel bad about myself? and I dont need that in my
life.

27. Nov. 19.28

Uve still a lot 2 learn about women :) well this particular model anyway. I know Ive issues about giving all of myself in a relationship. sorry but it takes a while. that's just the way I am. but u shud know I think being with u is really fantastic. all hush hush and secret and really risky.

. . .

28. Nov. 11.23

Gr8 it went so well at the doctors. ur heart always seems bulging and strong 2 me :)

. . .

29. Nov. 15.28

It was crazily hard not being able 2 touch, but of course I cant when Lærke is there, probably wudnt dare either – my body's a bit tender 2day – high tension due 2 lack of wet kisses on naked skin. soooo looking forward 2 seeing u without Lærke dragging at my heels.

29. Nov. 17.02

Im totally convinced we can work all this out. ecstatic at being ur pupil :) I cant imagine us ever not wanting 2 c each other. have a gr8 trip 2 Moscow!

29. Nov. 23.28

So have u told ur son Jeppe about us? :) cudnt stop urself? OK fine! :) but pls dont tell anyone else! and I mean that.

. . .

DECEMBER

1. Dec. 12.13

I should be in ur hotel keeping ur bed warm for
u – Im there in my dreams :) Im desperate for ur
overwhelmingly erotic passions. I feel were very
close even tho ur in Moscow. Im following the strict
instructions u left.

1. Dec. 16.10

Im totally fraught by this point – have been stuck
in meetings since this morning, constantly wet and
obsessing about ur smses. licking and sucking u and
feeling u inside me. its no longer a dream now. nearly
safe 2 start believing next week will actually come.

1. Dec. 16.28

My need for our lovemaking is so extreme Im having out
of body experiences.

1. Dec. 16.58

That sounds really out there. then try 2 imagine me on
top of u and under you and then from behind – wide
open. think gushing wet and wild. and that I melt in sheer
ecstasy as u thrust into my body.

1. Dec. 23.31

Nite nite hunkster. if only I was lying under ur warm
duvet. kisses.

. . .

2. Dec. 13.25

Mmmm yes. my lips and tongue played with ur gorgeous
cock for hours and we fucked again and again. and then
we came together as we kissed ferociously.

. . .

3. Dec. 16.04

Trying my damdest 2 read an MS here in the office,
but it has some passionate sex scenes in it and I keep
mixing up the characters with us. think I better go out in
that snow storm b4 I lose it altogether.

3. Dec. 17.42

Strangely enuff I am not shamefully horny. just VERY
horny :) hope u guys have a great party.

3. Dec. 21.18

I would love 2 come over and pleasure u for a whole day
next week. and remember 2 have a Wodka on me :) :)

. . .

4. Dec. 09.42

Hey u my hunk of a culture warrior on the Russian front. only saw ur message late last night and didnt want 2 disturb ur dreams :) hope they were sweet :) I spose ur eating kefir for breakfast. its said 2 b very good for u? think about last friday all the time and am full of longing.

4. Dec. 15.16

Bit by bit Im losing control. I long for u and ur bed all the time, just 2 make love and 4get everything else.

5. Dec. 00.35

Really missing u badly. and am fairly fkin drunk rite now. c u very soon baby sleep well. kisses.

. . .

6. Dec 10.06

Thnx a million 4 yesterday – it was short but exquisitely intense. in fact we kud easily have taken a bit more time. anyway I can still feel u had a massive come :)

6. Dec. 13.56

Remember 2 let me know when uve a day off. it wud b wonderful 2 just spend the whole day in ur bed.

6. Dec. 18.05

Wednesday is a good day 2 meet . . .

. . .

7. Dec. 15.11

Yes I spose u have 2 organize all ur other lovers? :)
whens best for u? around 10? then I can just roll out of
bed when the next one turns up :)

7. Dec. 15.18

Ah sry if I upset u. was only joking but gr8 2 know Im the
only one. and you have absolutely no cause 2 b jealous
of Gustav. our marriage is a sham. I mostly sleep on
the sofa – and when I do sleep in our double bed Lærke
lies in between us and nothing happens. I mean nothing
happens! the whole thing has been reduced 2 nothing
more than a latté together in a cafe with Lærke tagging
along :)

7. Dec. 15.26

Its best if ur not 2 tired when I come over. I really need
every ounce of ur love and tender care :) Im off 2 an
Xmas party and will try my best not 2 end up sozzled in
the usual glögg and boozefest.

. . .

8. Dec. 20.46

Hope I didnt overstay my welcome 2day J. with or
without clothes. its lethally delicious being with u.

8. Dec. 22.16

At last Ive read Jong all the way thru – the narrative
with Isadora and Adrian doesnt end right: she finally
determines 2 live out a fantasy shes had 4 a year and
follows him. but then his cock goes soft as frog spawn
and she gets dropped. tragic :-O :)

8. Dec 22.55

Ur dead right – frog spawn duznt sound very enticing :)

. . .

10. Dec. 23.30

Yeah. bit amazing but Im head over heels 4 u too and I
don't really know what 2 do tbh.

10. Dec. 23.48

Thnx J. then that makes two of us. u really r gorgeous.
Xmas is impossible tho. have 2 go 2 V and c the folks.
the usual family thing with Lærke and Gustav, would
much rather b lying in ur bed. just me an u in the whole
world. kisses.

11. Dec. 00.02

Do u really mean that? can I just move in with u and
bring Lærke with me? u really r a brilliant guy. but how
could we keep that secret? :)

. . .

11. Dec. 12.30

Im coming over at 2pm. getting horny just at thought of it.

1. Dec. 19.47

Thnx a million 4 a fucking fantastic afternoon. sooooooooo looking forward 2 the next one.

11. Dec. 19.58

Glad ur pleased I shaved my pussy – that was mainly 4 ur benefit. but its far more sensitive that way as well :)

. . .

13. Dec. 19.45

Missing u, kisses :)

13. Dec. 19.55

Hey I forgot 2 ask how u got on with the heart specialist?

13. Dec. 20.05

More tests? hope its nothing serious.

13. Dec. 23.26

Ull be fine im sure. sweet dreams baby. kisses.

. . .

14. Dec. 16.54

H as in hot and horny.

14. Dec. 19.25

As Im sure ur aware – Bologna is an abbreviation for
Brilliant Oralsex Longer Orgasms Guaranteed Nearly
Always. sounds a bit trashy I know. but its actually true.

. . .

16. Dec. 14.07

Hope u never ask me 2 disappear – that would
devastate me. thnx for a wonderful email. that was more
or less what I dreamed – thnx 2 Galeano and 2 u :) p like
porno in Pisa :)

. . .

18. Dec. 14.12

Lærke was talking about u today. it was a bit weird.
she really likes u. u get on very well 2gether and that
makes r relationship a lot easier. soooo looking forward
2 seeing u.

. . .

19. Dec. 12.30

Of course I'd love 2 go with u. but probably in a rather
less frantic version :) think Id like 2 go the whole way
with this: excitement. falling in love – total abandon,

deep affection – its an exhilarating roller coaster ride
:) but unfortunately any trip like that is just impossible
round Xmas. kisses.

. . .

20. Dec. 10.40
Yes Im almost myself again :) hope I wasnt 2 soporific
yesterday! when r we going 2 c each other?

20. Dec. 19.08
On my way in five.

. . .

21. Dec. 10.40
Ive had the most chaotic morning. dreamed about u last
night and overslept precisely because I was lying there
thinking of u. things just got more out of hand after that.
but now Im back on my perch fortunately and am fine
again :)

21. Dec. 11.57
One of my work colleagues has just been given a
company ipad and out of the blue a madly jealous
materialistic devil has sprung up in me – they shud give
me one as well goddammit! :)

21. Dec. 16.20

Hi gorgeous :) am utterly desperate 2 pull out of all this Xmas craziness and just be alone with u.

21. Dec. 23.40

R u still up? :) have just sold B and M 2 France, thats the 3rd sale this week. klass or what? r u heading 2 J tomorrow?

22. Dec. 01.17

Nite nite baby. PS Petra stopped me as I got into a taxi and started trying 2 tongue me ffs! :) but Im urs and urs alone.

22. Dec. 01.35

funny u shud say that cuz she reminds me of a maneating plant as well. except she's a lesbian! – anyway shell never get a chance 2 eat me :)

22. Dec. 01.45

Sleep tite my hunk. Kisses

. . .

22. Dec. 14.57

Yeah were really busy here – so Im stuck at my desk hammering away – as usual. Still dont know 4 sure whether I will have 2 work tomorrow.

22. Dec. 16.16

We can rendezvous first thing tomorrow if ur at home?
kisses :)

. . .

23. Dec. 09.06

Sorry hon but have 2 go straight 2 work after all. have
2 tie everything up before the Xmas break. a total pain.
and then its hit the road 2 V. – but in ur arms is where I
wanna be! still it wont be long till we c each other again
:) kisses and hugs from ur babe :)

23. Dec. 09.30

Did u cancel a meeting specially 2 c me? really sorry
about that J so sorry. think u know how much Id prefer
2 b with u. but theres Lærke 2 think of as well . . .
xxxxxxxxx.

23. Dec. 16.46

Ah gr8. Ill let u know very soon exactly when Im coming
back 2 town :) a shower of kisses 4 my adorable hunk.

23. Dec. 17.56

Finally battled my way out 2 V. talk about winter weather!
but its magical here. all snowy white and beautiful. ur
kisses are tingling all over my body and even tho ur
far away from me hope u can feel my urgent need for
ur mouth on my skin and all the other things we do.

the more immoral and amoral the better. from me 2
unbelievable u.

. . .

24. Dec. 21.34

Im sure its fabulous where u r. Here things are just like
always. weve nearly finished Xmas dinner and dads just
opened a champagne bottle with a dagger. right now
a goldfish is staring at me. outside its enchanting but
makes me miss ur kisses even more guy!

24. Dec. 21.34

Oh and course – really happy Christmas baby :)

25. Dec. 02.15

Hope uve had a good eve/night :) now have 2 get some
sleep. Lærke got way too many presents! but poor me
got next 2 nothing – lifes a bitch then u . . . kisses :)

25. Dec. 02.34

4got 2 say hope u have wonderful dreams. only about
me please. and not a stitch on us r between us.

. . .

25. Dec. 10.56

While u slowly peeled off my jeans and sweater and
then finally my panties u kept on kissing me all over. u

sucked and licked me and got so stiff u kudnt wait and had 2 fuck me hard. so you did that 4, like, ages. soft and hard and wet and hot . and as many kisses as stars.

. . .

26. Dec. 10.26
Kisses and more kisses 4 u :) on the way home now and well hopefully b entwined very soon!

26. Dec. 13.13
Mad 4 u!

26. Dec. 14.43
Whoo. just read Patti Smith's book in one go and now my eye makeup is all streaked. really outstanding but very sad. Wwhat r ur plans for the next few days?

26. Dec. 17.32
Tomorrow around half past nine?

26. Dec. 21.00
Brilliant :) its a date :)

. . .

27. Dec. 14.08
Yet another fking fantastic day with u! xxx! I could really feel that u missed me. the same way I had u.

. . .

28. Dec. 14.22
What about a cup of tea at urs?

28. Dec. 14.38
Within the next 10 mins. OK?

28. Dec. 18.12
On the way down ur stairway it hit me like a bolt from nowhwere – Im pregnant. I've just taken the test and its like sooooo positive? we have 2 get it sorted asap. am both shocked and kind of so what at the minute.

28. Dec. 18.20
OMG Im pregnant. I know it!

28. Dec. 18.37
Can we meet 2 discuss. like, very fkin soon?

28. Dec. 18.56
Yeah. in an hour? is that OK?

28. Dec. 23.58
This is mad stuff all this :) but Im delighted ur dealing with it the way u r – yes I understand u r totally against me getting rid of it and I luv ur tenderness and keen intelligence – but Im just trying 2 b realistic. and yes ur right that it would mean the end of all our sneaky

backdoor stuff. and I would really love 2. but on the other
hand . . . thats a good idea 2 speak 2 a gynecologist. so
I dont drag my own doctor into it. I think Ill go in and do
some work 2morrow up 2 lunchtime, so u can ring me
there. sweet dreams darlin. kisses :)

29. Dec. 00.03
Really really need 2 b with you right now.

. . .

29. Dec. 10.51
I took another test there now. 2 stripes again that
means, like, very pregnant. I didnt sleep a wink
last night. funny how such a tiny thing can set off a
tsunami of thoughts. Im doing OK thats all. just trying 2
remember that it will all be over with this time next week!

29. Dec. 11.22
Yeah babe. I think I could do that. maybe "our" cafe in
the center of town?

29. Dec. 11.46
Good idea – 2pm?

29. Dec. 16.59
Ive got this massive desire 4 us 2 ferociously fuck each
other. I really hope u want me that way too. can we make
a date for half past nine tomorrow morning in ur bed?

29. Dec. 17.32

I know its completely off the wall right now – but Ive a
mad urge 2 do all kinds of experimental sex with u :)

29. Dec. 18.35

I want 2 lie completely still and be gripped by u as u bite
my nipples really fucking hard. u have 2 go down on me
and lick and eat me till I come and then restrain me. I
mean this. and then fuck me hard hard and long.

29. Dec. 20.33

Its a deal :) hope extreme sex is the best way 2 blank my
mind thru all this!

30. Dec. 00.45

Ive just got home now. Ill be at urs tomorrow round 10.
kisses.

. . .

30. Dec. 15.16

Ive such an incredible urge and need 2 b with u at the
moment that leaving ur apartment was very difficult. the
thing that makes this abortion so hard is that I actually
believe we kud make a go of it and Im absolutely sure
we wud be really good together.

30. Dec. 16.35

Thnx yes. thats exactly what we would be. us two – me and u.

30. Dec. 17.15

Im getting waves of sickness and feel ready 2 faint. This is a very stubborn little seed uve planted in me! but I have 2 pull myself 2gether now. comfort food! gonna make some nigiri sushi with wasabi and pickled ginger and Ill keep Lærke happy on cupcakes.

30. Dec. 19.58

That was actually a brilliant meal I made – I must do it for u sometime. and yes its true weve really clicked as a couple :) our lovemaking was phenomenal today – I shud have just stayed put in ur bed.

30. Dec. 20.18

Am I rite in saying that a woman's cunt has the same consistency as a scallop? u of course r the expert? :) raw sushi served on my naked body is a deal but watch those chopsticks! :)

30. Dec. 23.52

Nite nite hunkster :) kisses. sleep tight

. . .

31. Dec. 11.56

Is that all? :) I thought u were older than that. seeing as
u were keeping sshtum about it :) miss u.

31. Dec. 12.58

Anyway, I think its just gorgeous 2 b with a more
experienced man who still manages 2 b a totally sexy
hunk :)

31. Dec. 13.21

After spending six weeks as ur pupil its hard 2 shock
me now :) ud need a bit more than that anyway :)
champagne and . . . in ur bed – now Im getting wet
again.

31. Dec. 19.07

Just ferried Lærke across town 2 a party. aside from u
know what, meeting u has been my year's biggest event
:) Im heartbroken we cant be with each other 2night but
hope u have a great evening.

31. Dec. 23.48

Hope ur enjoying the party baby :) all good here but
totally weird 2 b going round pregnant with ur child! but
everything will be fine. Im also missing u madly. think of
me and u in the new year and SMILE :)

. . .

JANUARY

1. Jan. 12.42

Dear darling gorgeous lover. HAPPY NEW YEAR. hope that party was a good start 2 the new year for u? kisses :)

1. Jan. 14.12

Am I really number one in ur life? :) I need a long naked hug from u – and u can tell me that everything is going 2 b all right – and then you will fill me up with ur kum :)

1. Jan. 16.20

Just back from Emmerys deli. got linseed bread, tapenade and chipotle pesto and went right past ur apartment – felt a violent urge 2 run upstairs 2 u.

. . .

2. Jan. 22.02

Just googled medical abortion. it sounds way too clinical and not at all pleasant!

2. Jan. 22.21

I really am delighted at the way ur dealing with this pregnancy and its a great relief ur coming 2 the clinic with me tomorrow. especially cuz I know ur not exactly thrilled with what Im doing. but on the other hand Im

soooo looking forward 2 us being able 2 fuck each other
once again without this thing hanging over us :)

. . .

3. Jan. 23.12

Thnx for sharing a weird day with me J. a strange
mixture of sadness and joy. the joy came in the way
it brought us closer 2gether – so at least it proves
something good can come from a terminated pregnancy.

3. Jan. 23.59

Yeah there r so many emotions :) sweet dreams baby
darling. am really mad about u. kisses 4 u and ur
wonderful body. am I still number one?

. . .

4. Jan. 10.30

Yeah – Im OK. nothing much happening, other than
my breasts are really sore and tender. thinking of u non
stop.

4. Jan. 14.01

Now Im really in a lot of pain so I better go home. rite
now I could do with a long wet zinging kiss from ur sweet
lips.

4. Jan. 15.37

Thnx :) I need 2 feel ur skin next 2 mine as well!

4. Jan. 23.41

Pills still havent kicked in ffs. nite darlin. Im completely
head over heels 4 u.

. . .

5. Jan. 09.49

Nothing unusual happening 2 me yet . . . is it OK if I
come over 2 u when Im done here? I dont want 2 b here
and definitely dont want 2 b on my own.

5. Jan. 10.01

It will be a few hours yet. I reckon. Ill be leaving here
around 1pm. is that OK 4 you?

5. Jan. 19.30

It was brilliant 2 b with u. but I really need 2 spend even
more time with u. getting a bit desperate 2 b honest.
what r we going 2 do?

5 Jan. 21.24

I know I know! and believe me Im thinking about both
things :) even though Ive been bowled over by stage 2
of ur love and passion helter-skelter ride. Im not exactly
sure where Im at. what level r on urself oh sex God?

5. Jan. 22.28

Ok, were on the same page then. I just read that as
being a bit dismissive of me tbh. I say that Im madly in
love with u and ur answer is that ull give me a photo
of urself for my purse. not exactly the most ferociously
passionate answer :) I hope its not cuz ur more
disappointed I chose 2 have an abortion than ur letting
on?

. . .

6. Jan. 10.26

Yes :) or rather no! pills still not working. glad Im going 2
the clinic at H again today. dreamed about u last night.
we were somewhere abroad and spent the whole time
wrapped around each other

6. Jan. 11.09

The truth is that Ive been insanely obsessed with ur
cock since yesterday. dying 2 lick and suck u until u hot
spurt in my mouth.

6. Jan. 11.46

I just completely melt when u touch me. my body is urs.
do what u want with it. I dont care. being tied up and a
slave 2 ur slightest whim sounds irresistible :) Im in :)

6. Jan. 12.37

OK. now its finally started – woosh.

6. Jan. 15.13

So now u have 2 give me a few days, but itll be worth
the wait cuz after that Ill be completely fuckable again :)

6. Jan. 15.20

I cant stop thinking about r lovemaking. its gr8 Im good
at multitasking. otherwise Id be fucked, or not as the
case may be! having really extreme and erotic fantasies
about us 2 in Paris – Last Tango.

6. Jan. 15.39

We r only so good together naked because were just as
good together with clothes on. like peas in a pod. perfect
fit baby.

6. Jan. 15.44

As an excuse for my constant horniness I plead a huge
surfeit of hormones running round my body ur Honour! :)

6. Jan. 16.00

Im just trying 2 explain my perhaps slightly surprising
behaviour. but its difficult – because it wont change the
fact that Im still horny as fuck.

6. Jan. 16.11

Oh yes. It has everything 2 do with u actually. havent I
said my body is urs but I know u can feel that.

6. Jan. 16.25

I love the fact u like my body – even tho I think my breasts are a bit on the shrunk side. when I was younger they were really lovely bloomers but as u know breast-feeding is a killer. Id have liked 2 have been a bit taller as well.

6. Jan. 22.25

I actually sat down and worked it out properly and in fact u r only number 16.

6. Jan. 22.30

Total abandon and multiple orgasms like bang bang bang? ha. I wish! no on that score u r one of the first. totally tragic that its nearly always so difficult.

6. Jan. 23.08

Nerudas The Captains Verses? I havent read that love poetry – but no probs cuz u can read it out loud 2 me ☺ and I was really young when I read Rimbaud. May b it wud b interesting 2 read him again. Mallarme tho is still one of my favourites.

6. Jan. 23.53

Yeah that was a big leap forward. needed 2 realize that teenage stuff, things going off the rails and Rimbaud are all of a piece 4 me.

6. Jan. 23.55

I had so many ambitions when I was younger but usually
seemed 2 hit a brick wall. need more time with u and 2
discuss things. everything under the sun with u. sex and
discussions strengthen each other.

7. Jan. 00.05

Im sure well work it out! nite nite baby :) kisses :) u know
that I long for ur body heat!

. . .

7. Jan. 16.00

I just want 2 b with u. end of and simple as. I dont care
where or how. so again were on the same page. and if
we just stay in bed or other places where we can fuck
freely we wont even need 2 travel very far :)

7. Jan. 16.41

A cornucopia of kisses and sex and floods of chilled
champagne. 36 hours is nowhere enough baby. we need
at least 50! is this at ur place?

7. Jan. 20.16

But it would be so cool 2 travel together cuz at least then
we could step out arm in arm into reality without having
2 worry about Gustav and Lærke. now I just need 2 find
some plausible excuse 2 get away

7. Jan. 21.18

By the way hon. Ive been invited 2 Petras 2morrow 4 dinner and I cant get out of it, even tho Im not that keen. but Im all urs on Sunday 4 the whole day. Yay! if u want me that is :)

7. Jan. 22.58

I have Lærke from 5pm but am OK b4 then. Id love 2 meet over green tea 2morrow but then its kiddo tagging along as well?

7. Jan. 23.09

Have 2 get Lærke 2 ballet classes right now but what about around lunch time? what suits u best? I think we shud just find a place somewhere round Østerbro?

7. Jan. 23.40

Now that sounds like a grrr8 idea! cu soon baby. kisses all over ur hunk body, especially ur really sensitive places :)

. . .

8. Jan. 17.57

Im thrilled u dont feel Lærke is a pain or gets in the way.

8. Jan. 18.12

Im sure u understand the kind of head wrecking questions Im struggling with right now over divorce etc.

and u have 2 b completely straight and honest with me.
otherwise Im going 2 go under in all this. Ive a very
strong feeling ur seeing another woman. Ive felt it ever
since we met yesterday. Jonah. r you seeing another
woman?

8. Jan. 18.51

No. that's no kind of answer. at the start of all this u kind
of gave hints that I might not b the only one and Im just
not sure if thats still the case. so no my q is absolutely
not crazy.

8. Jan. 20.55

Thnx a mill for that J. I really needed 2 hear you say it
loud and clear. Im really overjoyed u still want me and
Lærke 2 move in with u, but I still dont know u that well.
and anyway Im a bit all over the place at the minute and
here u r turning my life upside down . . . I know theres no
point saying this now but Ive a terrible feeling I rushed
into that abortion way too quickly.

8. Jan. 21.14

Yes OK. I actually do really regret it but we can put that
right baby.

8. Jan. 21.28

If wed decided 2 keep the baby, then of course it wud
have been the right thing 2 do. tbh Im trying not 2 dwell
on it 2 much. funnily enough theres something lovely 2

about standing on shaky ground together. we'll work it
out. no?

8. Jan. 21.46

By the way, Lærke was a bit funny today. I think u may
be rite that she senses something or other is going on.
so I take ur point. Im going 2 stop trying 2 have whole
discussions by text. just makes me really paranoid about
everything anyway. is noon tomorrow OK?

. . .

9. Jan. 17.42

Trying my best 2 read a script but cant concentrate cuz
keep thinking about how it wud be – me and u living
together!

9. Jan. 19.02

Its unbelievable how uve got me 2 overcome so many
bodily hangups and barriers :) so yes I just love, love
the fact Ive got a really neat little bite mark on one of my
breasts.

9. Jan. 20.15

I really adore lovebites. its no time at all since we
were last together but Ive already got serious physical
withdrawal symptoms – need 2 get very very close 2 u
again baby.

9. Jan. 20.50

I cant stop thinking about u!

. . .

10. Jan. 11.00

Wud b much better if I had a duvet impregnated with ur scent. or even better – that u actually were my duvet :)

10. Jan. 12.42

That sounds a bit weird – that u sense I need my space 2 think – hello!? do u not really mean its u who needs space? if u want we can just avoid contact 4 the rest of the week?

10. Jan. 13.38

Dont forget it was u who said just 2 days ago that I shudnt start big discussions by text and now u r doing it urself.

10. Jan. 13.46

U r being a bit unfair on me baby :(

10. Jan. 16.15

Im coming now.

10. Jan. 19.24

My inbox is spammed up with meaningless mails and
my body starts aching at the very thought I have 2 travel
for a couple of days. because what I really want more
than anything is 2 just hide in ur bed, close my eyes and
be with u and ur kisses.

10. Jan. 20.10

Yes! that's exactly what I need! making love totally
crazily and then gently beneath the stars. and u have 2
tie me 2 ur bed, so that Im urs alone and the rest of the
world doesnt matter. just disappears

10. Jan. 20.37

Yes. I want 2! Im already almost there as much as I can
be :) did u notice u called me ur girlfriend today?

10. Jan. 20.58

Yeah – I was like totally made up and proud :) because
its u I want and preferably inside me right now! ur hands
all over me. I feel you. and then we both just melt into
each other right at the same time. wow :-O

10. Jan. 21.00

My body is still a bit wonky tho – like I have a mild
hanging nausea. I think it must be physical symptoms of
falling in love.

10. Jan. 23.19

Hope you still have the faint afterscent of me in ur
sheets :) nite nite baby – kisses.

. . .

11. Jan. 08.52

Well so far everythings running 2 plan here :) see u early
tomorrow. for a few hours anyway. only if it suits u of
course?

11. Jan. 16.49

Hey my gorgeous hunk. Im lying on a hotel bed thinking
of u – a real shame ur not here rite this second cuz Im
building up very quickly 2 doing a hand job as I imagine
u fucking me :) everything going smoothly here. Tho
these company suits r a lot less sophisticated than I
thought. Im navigating my way round them better than
expected tho :) dying for u ridiculously madly! kisses
baby.darlin

11. Jan. 17.03

In my fantasy Ive ripped down ur pants and take ur cock
in my mouth . . . mmm :) but unfortunately I have get
back 2 a pile of manuscripts. FML! :):)

11. Jan. 18.37

Youll all have a great time Im sure :) were going off 4 a
meal at Julius Fritzner but I doubt if well stay out late.
even tho it will probably feel like that. xxxxx.

11. Jan. 23.54

We ate an insane amount of oysters and sushi, also drank exclusive champagne, and on the 1st of May I start my new job on the editorial team! :) and I think of u at least 5 times a minute . . .

12. Jan. 00.45

Yes one of the editors finally. at long last theyve twigged Im actually quite talented :) I reckon my salary will go up as well :)

12. Jan. 01.06

Thnx hon. xxxx :) dont worry 2 much about putting clothes on before I come round tomorrow evening :)

. . .

12. Jan. 10.31

Yes Im totally fuckable! and dripping wet 4 u

12. Jan. 11.36

Were just taking a break. cant stop thinking of ur hot naked body and u ramming me as u bite my breasts. u know I love doing it that way. yes I know all very base and shallow in the middle of these contract negotiations about serious amounts of money. but megagorgeous! :)

12. Jan. 14.44

Ive just come from a really bizarre meeting. this had 2 do with a novel about infidelity and the main character sounded like me! and then this guy started telling me about this fella hed met at another publisher's seminar but he kudnt remember his name. anyway it was as if he was describing u down 2 a T! how weird is that?

12. Jan. 18.47

Am in the plane now. nothing but totally yuk sandwiches in the airport Im afraid – if u have fresh rye bread that would be only superb. kisses.

13. Jan. 00.07

No I'm not jealous at all actually. and of course if u want 2 meet up with ur exes, lovers etc go ahead. u can even meet possible girlfriends 2 come for all I care. I just want 2 know who u really r and what way u think so I can know u even better.

13. Jan. 00.25

Gonna have a quick shower now. unfortunately it means our erotic scent and juices will be washed away :(

. . .

13. Jan. 13.04

Have a gr8 trip 2 Iceland! its blowing a gale out there so watch ur step baby.

13. Jan. 16.41

Are u ignoring the texts I sent u last nite or what? u know very well thats a sore point for me!

13. Jan. 17.50

Still no answer. will u pls tell me who + what actually means anything 2 you?

13. Jan. 18.10

Why the fuck r u not answering me?

13. Jan. 20.36

Thnx for ur answer. it makes me really proud and glad that ur going 2 let me in on more of ur thoughts and feelings and Id like 2 hear even more. of course like everybody u have a rite 2 ur inner secrets. as long as theyre not there as a barrier against me. u know very well Im totally besotted with u. the closer I can get 2 u the better.

13. Jan. 20.49

Yes its true we r groping r way 4ward a little bit. but thats OK precisely because we r standing on shaky ground. u need 2 know u play a much bigger role in my life than I could ever have expected in such a short time. kisses baby no actually just one looooong wonderfully mad kiss :)

13. Jan. 21.10

You make me so happy. u fill me with passion, physical presence and tenderness.

13. Jan. 22.54

All of a sudden its turned into a really crap evening.
my guts are wrenching me J and Im lying in the fetal
position on the floor. its upset Lærke and shes asking
me weird questions about death and dying.

13. Jan. 22.58

Now shes just asked if its not time if I get another baby
in my belly. she wud luv that she says.

13. Jan. 23.10

What ur baby in my tummy whenever I want?

13. Jan. 23.17

Do u really mean that? a child with me. wonderful
declaration of intent :) shame its too late this time round.
but at least we know if it happens again we dont have 2
worry :)

13. Jan. 23.24

Ur making it sound as if it would actually b good idea for
us 2 have a baby and that makes me really happy. Im
using flat coca cola for this gut rot and really fkin hope it
works. I c u b4 me stepping out expectantly in2 the dark
Icelandic night baby :)

13. Jan. 23.46

Kisses, so many kisses just 4 u :)

14. Jan. 00.28

You understood didnt u that me + u having a baby would not be a problem – yes?

. . .

14. Jan. 08.56

Morning babe. Im really looking forward 2 seeing all ur pictures. I miss u terribly. u seem very far away and here is just empty if ur not close 2 me. want 2 wake up by ur side and sense ur soft skin next 2 mine.

14. Jan. 12.35

I was left numb with shock the first time I was up there. it was all so in ur face, magically beautiful and Lord of the Rings!

14. Jan. 12.59

Yeah babe! lets go 2 Iceland together! the northern part is just out there! I can show u round the whole island :) we'll hire a 4 x 4 with camper trailer and just let nature take us where it will.

14. Jan. 13.15

Sitting here in deep discussions with a publisher + just 5 mins ago closed a deal for the Hungarian market. would much rather be up in Iceland with u :) lots of wild empty places 2 make love al fresco :)

14. Jan. 13.19

Really looking 4ward 2 next weekend! :) Unfortunately I'll have 2 work for a few hours every day, but u know Ill work out ways 2 cut the hours right back.

14. Jan. 13.58

When do you get back?

14. Jan. 19.09

Missing you. but trying 2 focus on reading scripts ffs!

14. Jan. 19.19

Maybe we could do that J. but theres a bit of a marriage crisis building here ull be surprised 2 hear . . . we might need a serious talk on Sunday. but Ill let you know in good time.

14. Jan. 19.50

I cant get it 2 work. Ive tried everything.

14. Jan. 21.40

If I was lying in ur hotel bed waiting 4 u tonight it would be a long wet naked night.

14. Jan. 23.56

Fkin weird reading a novel about infidelity – its all a bit too horribly close 2 our thing, the woman especially is very like me. have 2 put it down and hit the sack. wrecked. kisses.

. . .

15. Jan. 12.06

Yeah. I AM actually screwy enough 2 arrange a
christening in a church right facing the gynee clinic in H.
:-O

15. Jan. 15.24

Did u hang up when I rang ur home? as if ur the one
having an xtra marital affair.

15. Jan. 16.54

Yeah were a bit wacky. both of us. but I'm fine with that
:) and I think the crazy idea we got close 2 needing baby
clothes will take a while 2 go away. miss you :)

15. Jan. 19.23

OMG guy. went 2 jelly when I heard ur voice. Deep thigh
quivering longing!

15. Jan. 19.46

Right there where you nailed me so hard and deep, and
I got so wet and thrashy you had 2 tie me down.

15. Jan. 20.28

Oh Jonah ur texts set off such mad desire in me. I want
2 make love with u right this second! I've got heavy bws
– bad withdrawal symptoms. tell ya, all next weekend its
sheer nakedness for us.

15. Jan. 20.31

Totally floated boat, sopping wet panties here!

15. Jan. 23.43

Yougoddambetwewill and I and can hardly wait! sleep good hunk features. and dream sweet dreams :) I mean about me! take me. Im yours. showers of kisses babe.

. . .

16. Jan. 11.39

Shame but this novel on infidelity isnt very well written. so now Im on a Norwegian crime book that has "deep" references 2 Christianity. oh man the whole weekends just been swallowed up in shite work. sulk. :(

16. Jan. 12.42

Well Im sending you loads of hot kisses and a blowjob :) that usually stops u thinking, at least while ur getting done. can I ring you a bit later?

16. Jan. 13.42

My gorgeous hunk of a man, try imagining loooooong wet, wild strawberry kisses, then my tongue gliding over ur chest, my fingers slowly but urgently searching 4 and then caressing ur balls, I cup ur balls oh so gently in my mouth. ur cock is rock hard and throbbing next 2 my face and I take it in 2 taste it. let my lips lightly massage all round ur tip. I lick and suck it and very soon ur whole length is deep in my mouth. my tongue playing with it. down further and then back 2 the tip till u start 2 arch and are ready 2 explode. but I wait till ur at the very very edge and then take it fully into my mouth again with my lips and mouth going up and down on you increasingly urgently and passionately and I love, love that moment when you let rip in one massive deluge of iron tasting cum in my mouth.

16. Jan. 18.43
Hey baby have you landed yet? do you want me 2 come over for a couple of hours?

. . .

17. Jan. 09.53
No? Why do u think Im annoyed? Have some fairly heavy marks on my body from yesterday :)

17. Jan. 22.29
Hey u :) I can see in my inbox I'll have 2 b in the office very early tomorrow. but well soon be together again anyway!

. . .

18. Jan. 09.42
Did you sleep good babe? my bodys already got withdrawal symptoms 4 you. kisses :)

18. Jan. 13.18

Thinking of u nonstop.

18. Jan. 15.54

I didnt know u were still going for tests J. Is it ur heart?
long as its nothing 2 serious. remember 2 watch urself
hon :) yeah. would LOVE 2 see u more 2 but theres
Lærke 2 think of dont 4get.

18. Jan. 17.54

I hope u saved all ur energy for me on Sunday – my
cycle is back regular and in full flow now ya see :)

18. Jan. 18.22

The coil. in a few weeks I think.

18. Jan. 23.39

Have now finally accepted Lærke isn't going 2 sleep
anytime soon, so weve been dancing round 2 J Joplin.
that should break her. sleep good hunk :)

18. Jan. 23.50

Take another little piece of my heart now baby :) love my
lava earrings by the way.

. . .

19. Jan. 15.38

I should be lying in ur bed right now!

. . .

20. Jan. 09.14

Just off 2 the clinic at H for checkup etc.

20. Jan. 15.34

Back at H. station. womb's clear and they managed 2
stick that copper thing up me no problem. kisses.

20. Jan. 16.13

Hopefully can tomorrow :) not allowed 2day cuz of
infection risk. mentally Im totally fuckable :)

20. Jan. 19.48

Sooooooo looking forward 2 seeing u tomorrow. its still
on, yes?

20. Jan. 20.27

Straight from work suits me best . . .

20. Jan. 20.58

Wonderful I can be with u 4 more than a couple of
hours. cava and sushi sound good 2 me :)

. . .

21. Jan. 14.09

I can feel you close 2 me again now. 2 much sex on my
mind 2 get any real work done :)

1

. . .

23. Jan. 18.14

Not that good tbh, missing u loadz J. no more than
5 mins after leaving I got it bad 4 u. like a big hole
somewhere in me. hope we can c each other tomorrow?

23. Jan. 19.44

Im sore in every muscle and joint and deep red track
marks on both elbows. Fkin hell u really hammered me
right thru this time man – awesome. thinking of taking a
sicky cuz of it. waddyareckon my chances?

23. Jan. 20.11

Just tender and wrecked in that special way u know?
But u reckon a group mail telling them Im taking a day
off cuz Ive done nothing but fuck all weekend is not on?
maybe take one of my family days then :)

23. Jan. 23.30

C u at 4 tomorrow then J. night darlin :) wish ur body
was here beside me. kisses.

. . .

24. Jan. 11.19

Im still delightfully tender – need a massage :)

24. Jan. 11.28

Got a puncture this morning so just have 2 work out how Im going 2 get across 2 u – have 2 be home by 6.

24. Jan. 20.42

OK from now on I promise 2 b less of a control freak – if I can :)

24. Jan. 20.50

What me never being dominant. At all?

24. Jan. 20.51

Well ull just have 2 force me then :)

24. Jan. 21.28

I'm at my best when Im lashing out at others, but thats the point :) Im ecstatic when u get me all nailed and pacified.

24. Jan. 22.56

After intense cupcake baking/devouring and lots of reading aloud, I finally got Lærke 2 sleep. miss talking 2 u.

24. Jan. 23.55

Very delicate kisses and soooooooooo not domineering :)

. . .

25. Jan. 13.05

Im thinking of u and have come over all warm and happy inside.

25. Jan. 14.58

Ah I would love 2 go 2 Latin America with u! just kidnap me. anytime u want :)

25. Jan. 15.15

I would sooooooo love 2 b ur significant other on that trip. we kud follow juan maderos footsteps – and hey if u kidnap me what choice do I have :)

25. Jan. 15.35

Was just cleaning my desk up and found this photo of me – thought u might like 2 c Her Weirdness in her full glory – I mean. check out the crazy forehead man!

25. Jan. 15.46

Yeah its nice u love seeing me naked – but this towering forehead gets hid! – its always embrarrased me. hope Lærke doesnt have the same hangup.

25. Jan. 19.34

:) hello! . . . still waiting 2 b kidnapped.

25. Jan. 23.54

I'm fkin crazy 2 b in ur apartment when u get home from
work! then a long naked night under ur duvet, but Ill have
2 make do with yet another night on the sofa :(

. . .

26. Jan. 12.59

Do u think u might have time 4 coffee later today J?

26. Jan. 13.08

No. Id just really like 2 c u but I spose yeah thats kind of
serious :) Ive got Lærke this afternoon so shed have 2
be there 2. That OK?

26. Jan. 22.19

Not enuff kisses and 2 short J – BUT really really mega
impressed that a wired child just before her feed time
doesnt scare u off :)

26. Jan. 23.52

Sleep good J :) getting ready 4 lovely salacious allnight
dreams here :) kisses.

. . .

27. Jan. 10.47

Have a really intensive working from home day tomorrow
+ was wondering if I can do it at urs? reckon I kud b

round at 9am. if ur usually gone by then I can pick up the key later 2day?

27. Jan. 14.12

Yeah weve ended in a bit of a complicated situation all right. but the regular absence makes the longing more intense J. like r bodies r constantly pulling towards a place they cant go.

27. Jan. 15.12

Collecting Lærke soon then home and the dutiful loving mum. 2morrow have 2 b back at 6pm. but spending the whole day at urs! klass or what :) will u b able 2 work at all knowing Im back at ur flat more or less naked?

27. Jan. 18.43

U r totally right J – I need lots of TEC (tender erotic care) right now. I need 2 feel you in me! Ill be going nuts waiting 4 u 2morrow till u get back and fuck me :)

27. Jan. 23.58

Miss u.

. . .

28. Jan. 08.49

Fraid I cant make it! :(hope u have a gr8 day.

28. Jan. 09.13

Im sore all over with longing 4 u ffs – so let me know if
ur not gonna b 2 late getting home. then we might have
some time together. yes?

28. Jan. 12.22

Yeah all these fkin logistics r like trying 2 tie spaghetti.
Im totally fucked off with it 2 dont 4get. but is two hours
OK? its up 2 u J.

28. Jan. 12.33

But I can only be at urs 4 2 hours. gustav has 2 go out.

28. Jan. 12.40

We can even c each other 2nite if that helps but I have
Lærke . . .

28. Jan. 19.05

Sorry about the bloodspots on the sheets J. honestly Im
fine and havent seen any blood anywhere else – I know
it sounds a bit weird but I love the fact Ive left some kind
of trace of me behind. but OK bloodspots is maybe a bit
gross!

28. Jan. 19.54

Hope u didnt get a fright J – its just my womb has taken
a bit of a hammering this last month :-O PS – bit weird 2
think were sitting on separate sofas a few hundred yards
from each other.

28. Jan. 20.21

U know Im nuts about u and I hope u can feel the constant stream of love from me 2 u.

28. Jan. 20.31

So Im hoping I soon become the worlds best sex goddess so u never get bored with me :)

28. Jan. 22.40

Hah! there's loadz Id have no trouble coming up with – eg wild sex romps over several days! :)

28. Jan. 23.19

Then u kud give me daylong Jonah Sex Techniques masterclasses :)

29. Jan. 00.01

If I kud do magic Id magic myself across 2 ur arms and bed baby! kisses.

29. Jan. 00.08

I love, love, love being held in ur hands :)

29. Jan. 00.14

Your scent is all over my body :)

. . .

31. Jan. 08.50

Have a safe trip 2 Spain baby and enjoy urself. kisses :)

31. Jan. 14.39

I spose we shud use the word mistress. I'm OK J. but a
bit down. maybe an allergic reaction 2 the IUD. my skin
feels like its burning up. but it kud just b lovesickness
breaking out. physically. really miss u loads :) and am
shockingly sad were not in Spain together :(

31. Jan. 15.18

Ugh jealous feelings. and I spose its lovely and warm
down there. I know ull b busy but enjoy it anyway hon :)
PS can stil feel u came loads in me yesterday! :)

31. Jan. 19.08

Clinging on 2 dreams of us two wrapped around each
other in ur bed.

31. Jan. 22.50

Awesome 2 hear ur voice J. I love it when u ring and say
its Jonah B calling – sounds all formal. as if I might not
know it was a guy I constantly long 2 b naked with :)

31. Jan. 23.51

Ur big in me. soft thrusts then hard – a looooooong wet
pulsing session and I hold back and hold back till I just
cant anymore and go off like an earthquake as you go

with me :) then just wrapped around each other totally fucked and blissed out falling asleep together.

. . .

FEBRUARY

1. Feb. 10.28

Morning :) my dreams were only a tiny bit racy – but yes
we kissed. a bit . . .

1. Feb. 16.25

kisses on ur mouth and other more secret places of
gorgeous, hunky u :) I would love 2 b ur intimate PA.

2. Feb. 01.22

I was obviously not meant 2 get a good night's sleep
tonite J . . . there was a little person who kudnt find her
pacifier. so here we r now watching donald duck after
donald duck oh yes not forgetting minions minions
minions. Hope u slept well babe with hot dreams about
me.

. . .

2. Feb. 13.46

Finally got some sleep between half past six and eight.
right now feel more kids is not an option! table swimming
with juice, goo, halfeaten fruit same old coffee and street
level grey clouds outside :) miss u and ur lovely food
arrangements like mad. kisses upon kisses.

2. Feb. 18.07

Im coming over after work on Monday. I have Lærke for a few hours and Im assuming thats OK?

2. Feb. 20.25

Well work it out :) it also depends on how u r which reminds me – when is it u go in 4 those tests again?

2. Feb. 23.15

After putting little angel 2 bed Im in my own warm bed now and trying 2 keep my housewife head on. soooooooo looking 4ward 2 seeing u again J! and ur hair :) kisses baby. GR8 ur coming home 2 me.

. . .

3. Feb. 09.16

Hi there :) yeah same 2 u baby. is ur flight leaving now? safe journey!

3. Feb. 09.42

Mmm how delicious. hope it was me u dreamed about! my pussy is wide open for u and wants ur rock hard cock up it 24/7 :)

3. Feb. 10.15

Now Im really fuckable! I wanna b fucked by u in every way and place possible. wanna taste ur cock. caress it with my tongue and take its cum deep deep in my throat.

and then I want u up my splashy hole. just promise 2 grip me like iron as you nail me.

3. Feb. 15.24
Working from home today and will soon have a manuscript 2 proof. sooooooo lovely knowing u r close by J. but a bit fkin frustrating I cant go over 2 u!

3. Feb. 19.19
Really! I could slip over 2 u right this second. ur like a magnet and I can feel ur pull so strong.

. . .

4. Feb. 11.01
Do u have time for coffee this afternoon J?

4. Feb. 11.54
Have 2 nip in 2 town and get a prezzy for Camilla but I can come over 2 u after. if ur back? – just think we should see each other?

4. Feb. 12.50
Our office kitchen is like so Jamie Oliver on a Friday – have just scoffed a huge soy burger and WAY too much creme brulee. :) c u at urs round half past four?

4. Feb. 13.25
Sounds a bit cold tbh J u going on about my usual

schedule :) but yeah I have 2 b home a bit after six.
babysitter changeover with Gustav. I come he goes . . .

4. Feb. 13.33
But I also want 2 see u 2morrow – late morning and then
b with u as long as u can and want 2.

4. Feb. 22.03
Good good :) c u soon. kisses :)

4. Feb. 22.49
Sounds like gr8 minds thinking alike J! nite nite baby.
sleep tite. kisses.

. . .

5. Feb. 09.28
10.30 :)

5. Feb. 10.44
Im down at ur entrance – will you buzz me in?

5. Feb. 16.24
It felt totally wrong 2 leave. just want 2 b with u.

5. Feb. 16.29
Megasorry the IU thingmy is jabbing u J. its defo coming
out again if I dont stop bleeding – don't worry well work
something out. where theres a willy :)

5. Feb. 16.59

I know. Ill get this coil checked. did I ever tell u by the way that Im crazy about u?

5. Feb. 17.23

Yes I am J – totally.

5. Feb. 23.04

Having a meal with x. and y. all very jolly and "oh its Camillas birthday! lets have fun." but drinking loads of cava and good laugh. very johanne! :) only thing missing is u :(

5. Feb. 23.43

Love, love that I still have ur body scent on me :) it wud b so nice 2 b able 2 warm u up in ur bed. well see each other as soon as u get back on Monday.

6. Feb. 00.58

Finally got home J. do u know what? Ive sat here ages looking at Lærke and wondering what a mixture of us 2 wud have been like. am I loony or what? nitey nite kisses.

. . .

6. Feb. 12.51

Im fkin crazy about u :) its all a bit mad but totally wonderful 2.

6. Feb. 21.23

Isnt it early 2morrow ur having that coronary arterio graph thing, or whatever its called – just googled, sounds heavy J! hope theyre taking care of my baby! kisses.

. . .

7. Feb. 13.09

Hope everythings gone as planned J. thinking of u nonstop. just let me know when I can come over.

7. Feb. 13.59

R u OK J? Im so grateful 2 them 4 looking after u so well! when u come home I can come over 2 u and pamper u. I miss u and really want 2 b there 4 u now.

7. Feb. 14.10

OMG J ur making me really nervous and scared! sorry but why do u need an operation – WTF?

7. Feb. 14.59

OK calmed down a bit have read loads on triple bypass ops now. looks heavy duty there in black and white + theres loads of medical terms I havent a clue about but as I read I can get a handle on it and remember Im here all the time 4 u. just wish I kud b by ur side right now J and do anything whatever whenever 4 u.

7. Feb. 15.05

Just say the word if u want me 2 come over 2 the hospital this evening!

7. Feb. 15.43

An ocean of soothing kisses for u :)

7. Feb. 17.49

My dear, dear gorgeous man. I want 2 b with u as soon as u get home and stay as long as u want me 2. my plan is all about getting u 100% again with loads of healthy sex and energizing raw food oh yes and more sex :):) showers of kisses. ring later if u can.

7. Feb. 21.30

It really pains my heart that ur hearts in pain J. even tho I know ur familys round u I know u also know Im there anytime 4 u 2 babe – ah Jonah I so want 2 kiss u all over and make u better! hugs :'(

. . .

8. Feb. 09.30

Good morning hon. hope ur night was as good as possible. Let me know when ur being allowed home. many many kisses.

8. Feb. 13.10

Im coming over in the afternoon J. then we can c if u
want me 2 visit later as well :) lots of caring kisses :):)

. . .

9. Feb. 09.50

Hope u feel much better after a good nites sleep babe.
miss u madly! kiss upon kiss.

9. Feb. 10.00

Most of all I want 2 b by ur side J. just talking 2 u looking
at u. but I cant godammit! Not this evening anyway :(
have 2 meet the girls early evening – but really want 2 c
u Thursday 2 Sunday next week if u can and r up 2 it?

9. Feb. 12.52

Ill c if I can get out 2 u b4 going home 2 Lærke. I really
need 2 lie close 2 u babe and make love with u – Im
going mad with horniness!

9. Feb. 20.55

One day u might long for the time when I didnt take up
so much room in the bed :)

9. Feb. 21.04

Pls don't think Im just coming 2 c u 4 sex! Noh! I just
want u so badly J! and u have 2 remember Ive never had
2 deal with a serious medical problem b4. so 4give me

if I do/say something wrong. tbh Im still a bit shocked +
unsure what helps best. it wud help if u told me exactly
what ur thinking?

9. Feb. 22.16

Yeah theres loads of obstacles rite now J :) if u get a
bit down about things u really need 2 share with me. u
know I really wanna be with u babe. and despite all this
chaos were in its still more and more wonderful being
us!

. . .

10. Feb. 11.44

Hey u! My favourite erotic man thing :) tell me how ur
bodys doing?

10. Feb. 13.39

U need 2 listen 2 ur body J baby. pamper urself and
take it really easy for a while. I have 2 head into town
2 choose some gifts for my present obsessed family
cuz they want a wish list from me. but I can be with u
tomorrow as I have 2 work from home – is that OK?

10. Feb. 18.11

Cudnt get round so good this morning cuz my key
broke in the bike lock ffs :(coming over 2 u tomorrow. is
everything OK? hope its not driving u fkin mad me askin
if ur OK all the time?

10. Feb. 20.39

Having a meal with Jeppe and Sara :) do u really mean that? both me and Lærke would love 2. but Im a bit nervous already. even thinking about it I mean – r u not?

10. Feb. 21.02

Terrified that they think Im a terrible person. but it might be OK and actually nice :) and suddenly all very official. not the big secret anymore. but that might also be a really good thing

. . .

11. Feb. 18.02

Be round in 15 mins. Have 2 get Friday treats first for Lærke – dried cranberry and blueberry and organic almonds.

. . .

12. Feb. 10.48

Thnx 4 yesterday J :) impressed u noticed Id removed my wedding ring – do u think Gustav will be mad at me? oh by the way, did I leave my script at urs? working on it at the mo, so Ill just get a shower and bike over 2 u in half an hour. assuming thats OK?

12. Feb. 13.38

Its so magic being with u! both with and without bathrobes :) kisses.

12. Feb. 14.16

Shit J really need my red pen. wud u have a look round 2 c if I left it behind?

12. Feb. 14.24

Thnx 4 all those wonderful orgasms you gave me hunkster! Im still so wet it feels like u just cum up me a second ago – but u came somewhere else of course :)

12. Feb. 18.21

Will b there in ten J. Lærke keeps asking does she still get her Friday treat?

12. Feb. 21:49

Always feel a big gap the second I leave ur apartment babe.

12. Feb. 23.34

Ill say good night then hunkster – even though ur sure 2 b asleep by now. thinking of u and ur illness a lot. I know + can feel it worries u J. but when I close my eyes and dream us dreams I know everythings gonna b good! loads of kisses :)

. . .

13. Feb. 11.47

Morning baby. hope ur good – but I get anxty when I dont hear from you. u know Im nuts about u :) lots of healing kisses!

. . .

15. Feb. 10.44

Hey hunkster! whats with the long fkin silence? :) everything OK? hope ur not about 2 disappear on me? I really need u – in lots of ways honey!

15. Feb. 11.14

Well my dad might be coming on a visit. maybe tomorrow evening. but if he doesnt turn up I'll come over :)

15. Feb. 14.22

Soooooooooo want 2 c u babe. but Im snowed under with work at the minute. not just scripts but loadz of practical things I just have 2 get done. but that doesnt mean u have 2 go AWOL on me! sure i know uve loads 2 think about and I wud far rather be with u 24/7 sharing ur sad and glad. but Ive no chance of ever doing that if u back off :-O

15. Feb. 15.57

Aww J honey! Ill be so touched and redfaced if u buy me a present. but FYI size 36 is a perfect fit, but Im more comfortable in size 38 if its tight fitting. Ask the assistant if in doubt :)

15. Feb. 16.05

And J dont u go betting with anyone about what size I am. I dont like that thing men do and it makes me feel shit and embarrassed! :(

15. Feb. 16.14

Dont laugh but Ive just eaten a shit load of chocolate and OK have mega munchies guilt. so defo size 38! :) kisses.

15. Feb. 16.22

Hey u! now I cant concentrate on my scripts and Im sitting here dripping for u and very fuckable. dying 2 b in ur arms as u fill me with ur cum.

. . .

16. Feb. 19.07

Pissed off today with all the little work tasks different people expect me 2 do even tho theyre actually NOTHING 2 do with my job. Like, Im sposed 2 b a LITERARY agent y'know? cant hide my annoyance sometimes – not good for my career I know – but fk it Im really looking 4ward 2 being with u tomorrow. u and me and these gorgeous black undies I got. me. u. black panties. and fk all else :)

16. Feb. 23.05

With ur supreme technique oh Sex God ull find a way of fucking me when theyre still on me! :) sweet dreams about me baby. have 2 do a few more hours with this fkn commercial book. mare of a job.

. . .

17. Feb. 11.22

Hey J! wasn't the deal that I wud be pampering u and looking after u?

. . .

18. Feb. 16.19

Ill be over in an hour.

. . .

19. Feb. 21.54

Is it OK if I come over 2 u in five mins.?

. . .

20. Feb. 14.51

Kud do with some fresh air right now – can I come and visit u or are u totally wrecked?

20. Feb. 15.06

I know! But I can get the fresh air on my way over 2 u :)
so . . . yes or no?

20. Feb. 18.59

The whole thing is really fkin complicated at the mo and
I hope u dont c me as the icecold bitch. u know very
well Im being stretched every way + trying 2 keep it all
2gether – Lærke, family, work, fighting 2 keep down
that worry in my guts. plus u know that I love 2 have
everything under control – and u? well I actually hadnt
planned that bit! :)

20. Feb. 20.50

I think the scariest thing 4 me would be total collapse.
and I dont want it 2 b just me that dictates our
relationship cuz u know that I want us 2 decide things
together.

20. Feb. 21.22

Yeah lifes suddenly all helter-skelter and its a bit
alarming! :) but I was serious that time when I said u had
none of the worry :) and I don't really have any right 2 lay
claims on ur life.

. . .

21. Feb. 15.17

No ur right. I dont know what ur going thru. but Im clear

that I dont want 2 b an added problem in ur life at this time.

. . .

22. Feb. 10.48

Have u reduced me 2 an erotic plaything? :) but J – I mean it when I say the moment u ask me Ill come 2 visit.

22. Feb. 10.59

No I know ur madly in love with me babe.

22. Feb. 11.32

No tomorrow I cant – were going 4 dinner straight after work. but what about Thursday?

22. Feb. 12.51

Anyway try 2 enjoy this time – lazing under the duvet, crap tv and gr8 books :)

. . .

24. Feb. 19.01

Yes I know I dont say much about ur operation but I worry quietly 2 myself tbh. Im trying 2 work out how best I can be there 4 u but its not easy J. ull tell me if I can do something. yes? really lovely 2 c u 2day and fkin genius u can get me 2 cum in that way! best orgasms Ive ever had :-O

24. Feb. 19.42

Even tho Im not as physically with u as Id really love 2 b, Im still totally with u in my mind + thoughts! :) and u know v well that right this nanosec I want u like mad! OMG

. . .

25. Feb. 23.53

Gr8 u haven't disappeared on me babe :) phew! seemed like u were ignoring me. saw a good play with Petra. now its minions at home ffs.

. . .

26. Feb. 09.29

Why has ur operation been postponed?

26. Feb. 10.12

Im going 2 c my parents but will be back 2morrow afternoon so we can b together when I get back? kisses.

. . .

27. Feb. 22.39

Its really horrible 2 suddenly have 2 part just at the
moment when were so tightly bonded :(

. . .

28. Feb. 11.37

Ive been just on the point of texting (sexting? :):)) u all
morning but info requests + questions keep raining down
on me and I have 2 answer there and then. Im making
a bid 4 a book as well. but I miss u like fk guy! really
awesome 2 c u yesterday! we just work as a couple!
simple as :)

29. Feb. 18.02

Hey my gorgeous man! enjoy ur sons birthday
celebrations today :) and be glad his year wasnt as
crrayzeeeee as mine :)

. . .

MARCH

1. Mar. 17.48

Really lovely that Jeppes Sara is pregnant. and yeah
imagine if he had a brother or sister (I wud NEVER use
the term "half" or step brother – YUK) that was more or
less the same age as the little new one they have on the
way. OMG I soooooooooo want 2 b naked with you! :)

2. Mar. 00.53

Been editing for seven hours non stop. nearly done now
and can reconnect with the outside world :) wonderful.

. . .

2. Mar. 11.36

I was just about 2 write u a panting hot email :) u wanna
c these panties Ive on me babe and my loins are aching
4 u. need hardcore erotic – need u 2 get wired into my
bod. my bod needs it bad babe – 4get the top half of me!

2. Mar. 14.06

R u doing good? What do u say 2 me coming over in the
afternoon?

2. Mar. 15.10

U sure thats a good idea babe? isnt it best if its just u

and Jeppe? U and ur son need 2 talk privately about
things surely? just before it happens I mean. when
exactly is the operation itself?

2. Mar. 15.27

Just soze I can be clear about this. ur being admitted
early tomorrow and have the triple bypass the day after
tomorrow – yes?

2. Mar. 15.39

I can feel my emotions rising the second I think about
the operation. so god knows what its like 4 u + Jeppe.
So I really thinks its best I step back and leave u both 2
it. will b holding ur hand in spirit tho J as the whole thing
progresses :)

. . .

3. Mar. 18.19

Im not going 2 that reading after all J. guests arrived
all of a sudden. so Ive made a big chili con carne with
chevre chaud salad. thinking of u 60 times per minute.
ring anytime u want if u want 2 talk. showers of kisses.

. . .

5. Mar. 13.21

Jonah darling :) I know u cant answer this right now
but Jeppe told me the whole thing went extremely well!

– fantastic! waddaguy! waddaheart! :) soooooooooo
looking 4ward 2 seeing u babe. countless kisses!

5. Mar. 13.44

Sooooooo lovely 2 hear from you. ur just gorgeous u
really r :) watch those morphine highs tho! :-O

5. Mar. 19.19

I am of course assuming ull let me know the second you
want me 2 visit!

5. Mar. 22.56

Aw J. r u in real pain hon? kills me 2 hear that! but I
spose its normal yeah? and in a way a gud sign that ur
healing. No? Im rite by ur side babe. soothing kisses.

. . .

6. Mar. 11.14

R u sure its OK if I bring Lærke along J? don't worry Ill
make sure shes quiet and sits still. Im getting a lift with
Jeppe and Sara – cant wait 2 c u. I wont have flowers
with me because I myself get sooooo down when they
start wilting.

6. Mar. 15.18

Back home now and Lærke keeps asking why Jonah
has yellow legs. what were those things on Jonahs
arms. why do they have 2 do something 2 Jonahs heart

:) really gr8 2 c u again J. sooooooo looking 4ward 2 the time when we can bonk again guy! remember Im here 4 u always babe.

6. Mar. 16.49
Im totally nuts about u. doesnt matter ur yellow and spaced on morphine!

. . .

7. Mar. 17.10
Is it OK 2 ring u?

. . .

8. Mar. 10.05
At work and its all gone a bit mental here. but Ill be home 2nite and we can talk any time :) how r u now?

. . .

9. Mar. 09.48
Is it still in the evening ur being discharged J? wud u like me 2 come by later? or r u 2 wrecked?

9. Mar. 11.17
J darling. my view is that uve really been thru the mangle emotionally and physically and uve also felt kind of pushed 2 the sides. u know v well that Im

sooooooooo dying 2 c u. BUT I also have 2 look after
a very demanding child + a stressful job – difficult
balancing act babe!

9. Mar. 19.48
R u sposed 2 b on ur own the way u r? or is Jeppe with
u? please dont b sad honey :) think u shud ring me
anytime u want. kisses and TLC hugs :)

. . .

10. Mar. 16.46
Out walking already. imagine! but u disappeared when I
went 2 get my bike ffs!

10. Mar. 17.30
But u know very well I never park my bike near ur
entrance. its always a bit round the corner. V important 2
remember its still a secret were an item! if u need some
air and another little walk later come over 2 me – ull be
very welcome.

10. Mar. 20.15
Just 2 let u know FYI – putting Lærke 2 bd 4 next half
hour :)

10. Mar. 20.36
She's asleep now :) so just come over when it suits!

. . .

11. Mar. 23.20

Thnx for an awesome evening hon :) ur strong but delicate hands and mouth turn me 2 jelly – and amazing u can get me 2 cum like that even when I have 2 b dead quiet soze not 2 wake Lærke. oh and I forgot my panties again and a few kids dvds so Ill get them tomorrow. kisses 2 my hunk of hunks :)

. . .

12. Mar. 22.48

U really mean so much 2 me – am still floating and fantasticly fuckable :)

. . .

13. Mar. 18.35

Ugh gross! Just seen pictures from that pussybox on the net. have u seen them yet J? dont get the funny with showin all those different cunts. real turn off and defo not 4 me. and if mine looks as gross as them Ill never let u take a picture of it. swear!

13. Mar. 19.30

I just think theyre disgusting and u cant say theyre exactly made for the camera! I actually had 2 peep at them thru my hands and look at them in small doses.

but OK. if ur a better pussybox artist than that website ur
welcome 2 snap mine :)

13. Mar. 19.42

Delighted you think my pussy is a lot prettier! cuz if it
wuz just as gross as the ones on that site ud soon get
turned off me :-O I just go wild when ur inside it. OMG
mad 2 kiss u all over and feel u taking me hard so I gasp
as ur nailing me.

. . .

14. Mar. 10.55

Ive still got a few windows 2 fill in my calendar 4 Paris.
but right now all I want is 2 get my hand in ur trousers
and get a really steamy kiss ffs!

14. Mar. 11.50

Im still waiting 4 ur answer J? – Ive tried 2 invite myself
a few times now havent I? cuz I sooooooo want 2 visit
u :) tried u last night but nothing. maybe u just need a
rest babe and thats fine but let me know when I should
come? kisses.

14. Mar. 13.47

Im wet and horny today too – so I think were back in
cycle hunkster!

14. Mar. 14.25

U r welcome 2 nail me. right now and always :)

14. Mar. 16.17

On the way over!

. . .

15. Mar. 11.01

I love, love that Im a part of ur training program in that
very specific way :) have 2 have a quick meet with Petra
at 5. so how bout round six?

15. Mar. 11.52

Blown away that uve risen 2 the challenge and
transformed urself into an innovative sex technician :)
Im right there with it as long as u promise 2 watch urself
:) double glad that it involves a duvet as it involves ur
rockhard kitchen table :-O

15. Mar. 22.14

Hope u werent left completely lamed by that heavy
blowjob J? :):)

16. Mar. 00.13

Nite nite gorgeous :) have a good resting sleep. lots of
TLC and loadzakisses from ur loving baby :)

. . .

16. Mar. 11.28

Sorry but havnt time 2 wreck ur body today. got friends arriving from Iceland + Norwegian, Finnish and French ones 2. making mussels in white wine with toast on the side. hoping 2 c u tomorrow before I head off 4 Paris.

. . .

17. Mar. 09.42

J did I leave a small shampoo bottle in ur bathroom, or did u throw it out? :) its perfect for travelling and I always fill it up. little things like that save so much hassle. can I come and get it about 1pm?

17. Mar. 18.28

Pulled a coat out that I havent worn in years and guess what the only thing was I found in the pockets? – ur business card! :) thought about throwing it away cuz I obviously dont need it anymore but kudnt do it. felt how lifechanging that card is. like, if I hadnt got that card J and not texted u afterwards . . . well we wudnt b where we are 2day! :)

17. Mar. 19.51

Yep. its staying in the coat pocket babe :) many passionate, horny and rather loving kisses from me 2 u :)

17. Mar. 23.44

Flight delayed because of all this snow ffs but got here and am now on way 2 meet Camilla at a bistro!

18. Mar. 00.13

Wow bit freaked out here J. had 2 stand waiting 4 quite
a while on a horrible dark station platform then even
more unpleasant train carriage. very dark and scary.
just heard 2 guys speaking Danish as I got off so Im
following them. hope they keep an eye out for me if
necessary :-O

. . .

18. Mar. 16.15

Hey! was just about 2 text u! Gr8 minds think alike!
longing 4 ur naked body :) soooo wish u were here J.
Then we kud have found some secret places away from
meetings where we kud kiss + do r thing!

18. Mar. 16.29

How u feeling? still any pains? maybe ur body's enjoying
the break from me? :) but for all I know ur bed might be
overflowing with naked women! :)

18. Mar. 16.38

Ok sorry J if u didnt think that was funny.

18. Mar. 16.51

Uve not even heard the end of the story by any means
J. I almost rang u last night. I was actually in tears cuz
I didnt know my metro line stopped running fairly early.
Camilla told me 2 just get off at Chatelet and take a cab.
there were no cabs anywhere so I had 2 hoof it 4 over

an hour. didnt get 2 the apartment until half past three in the morning. soooo did not need that! :(

18. Mar. 17.05

Have u seen all of Dexter now? I often think Im like that single mum hes doing a line with.

18. Mar. 17.32

Whoa standing next 2 O herself . . . in truth she looks a right mess :-O

. . .

19. Mar. 16.58

Everything OK J? ur being fairly quiet? kisses from ur baby :)

19. Mar. 17.10

AW J b fair! I didnt mean that bout women in ur bed and Ive already said sorry ffs.

. . .

20. Mar. 12.39

Be warned hunkster – Im dying 4 u!

20. Mar. 14.35

Well its not really a surprise that ur still in a lot of pain is it? I mean its only just a couple weeks since u had the operation. u need 2 b more patient darlin.

20. Mar. 23.14

So only a mad half day left and then on way home – yoohoo! :) hope ur better now babe! not long now. trillions of kisses!

. . .

21. Mar. 13.10

Ive just one more meeting in an hour and then Im going out 2 make the most of the sunny weather :) but u being pissed off with me and ignoring me just cuz Ive been away for a few days is not really nice j. its not as if uve missed out on loads of fun is it? well soon b back 2gether enjoying the spring sunshine :)

21. Mar. 22.41

J. u r a bit down at the mo which is understandable. but if u just go with the flow and enjoy each day of getting better and having all that time 2 urself ull get a gr8 lift babe! missing u soooo much :)

. . .

22. Mar. 01.07

Yes I'm close by again :) hope u and Jeppe enjoyed being together. nite nite kisses :) soon b in each others arms babe!

22. Mar. 12.41

Looking after Lærke on my own at the moment. gustavs
not here as usual. but I really want 2 come 2 u. but itd b
with Lærke tagging along. how does that sound?

22. Mar. 13.30

:) so cool u want 2 c her as well – u 2 really get on gr8
2gether – have 2 pick her up late afternoon and then
have 2 sort some really boring practical things 4 a while.
round half past six?

22. Mar. 22.37

Imagine if we kud just fuck each other the whole night –
thats only thing I actually wanna do. but its a mare 2 sort
with Lærke hanging round. just say if u get tired of me!
Im tired of myself ffs.

22. Mar. 23.04

Its both highly fkin frustrating and also emotionally
draining that we cant just glory and wallow in each other.
and imagine if she woke as we were hard at it. then Im
the worlds worst mother? But lets try it at least when
shes really deep asleep. We got away with it once b4 :)

. . .

23. Mar. 12.08

Hey u! Im getting fairly fkn desperate here and have 2

go on a short trip now – so an absolute age b4 we can
get it on ffs :(what can we do J?

23. Mar. 13.10

Tell ya guy. need sex with u soooooo much. goin crazy
here! need 2 work out how best 2 fuck u with Lærke
around. But at urs or mine? I know u cant relax as good
at mine. Gustav still living here and all that and u only
coming when hes away. Cumming! LOL

23. Mar. 23.20

Yeah OK maybe I go thru passive phases whereas, yes
its true, ur mostly proactive. but if ur still someone who
expects certain BIG things from me u need 2 know while
I cant deliver them right dis minute if ur a bit patient it will
b worth it I promise!

. . .

24. Mar. 12.50

I really really hope u still want 2 c me even tho I admit I
feel like Ive got "problem" stamped all over me. if u kudnt
be bothered seeing me anymore u have 2 tell me. u cant
just disappear on me ffs!

24. Mar. 17.32

Dont get that last message at all. r u saying I get off on
the whole logistics of it all and ticking the boxes? or r u
saying Im like that cuz Im madly in love? :(

24. Mar. 19.07

Well I cant see anything funny or jokey in it J – Im just trying 2 take care of myself not being a fkin accountant, logistics manager or control freak whatever ffs. now Im speechless. first time ever with u. I just dont fkin get how we move apart and get all defensive if we dont c each for a couple of days guy? :(

24. Mar. 19.32

Yeah. Im well aware ur still in a lot of pain and the op was a massive physical shock 2 ur body. but never b unsure of me J. never ever. pretty promise? hugs and kisses 4 my hunkster :)

24. Mar. 20.30

I havent rung cuz Ive been stuck in a fkin packed train since half past four. otherwise I wud have loved 2. Jesus of course I wud love 2 give u a blowjob right here + now. r u desperate rite this second? dont u want me anymore if I cant do things immediately?

24. Mar. 21.37

U need 2 always bear in mind J that I always look 4ward 2 seeing u – always. and that I long for u so much it makes me sore all over. what I wud love most of all is 2 just b able 2 live my life under ur duvet. me and u just together under the duvet and fk the rest of the world! :)

24. Mar. 21.46

Yes yes! always mad 4 u and ur hot bod under the duvet.
mental kisses ffs.

. . .

26. Mar. 16.36

Hey gorgeous u :) lovely day here. just went mad buying
a shit load of books. AND an ipad 2 whoohoo! yeah I
wud be a pretty adornment 2 ur bed rite now guy. as Ive
these waaaaaaaaaay sexy panties on :) can b lifted at
either side . . .

. . .

27. Mar. 10.37

Morning babe. hope u had a lovely long and restful night
with totes outrageous dreams about nakedness :) what
u up 2 2day? heading off 2 Aamanns deli for brunch
shortly with my workmate Petra. Im famished man!

27. Mar. 23.36

Back home now :) kisses all over :)

. . .

28. Mar. 12.04

Have u bought Dexter 4 yet?

28. Mar. 13.20

J. Ill do my very best 2 ensure we c each other asap. Im just totally buried in work at the mo. no smiley. sry.

28. Mar. 21.07

Babe. Im so sorry bout all dis. its just that everythings just so chaotic right now. plus Gustav is a bit knifeedge at the minute and I just got home from work. r u OK? have u ever felt like nothing fits together anymore and its all running away from u? and a body that aches all over. I miss u really fkin badly.

28. Mar. 22.15

Fuck! Gustavs behaving really weird at the mo J. maybe hes started wondering about us?

28. Mar. 22.24

Yeah but has he seen ur business card lying around or somethin? or maybe Lærkes said something bout u. WTF do I do J? if I suddenly turn up at urs with Lærke wud that b OK?

28. Mar. 22.35

J thnx so much 4 that. ur a star. hope Gustav calms down so a moonlight flit isnt needed! :-O

28. Mar. 23.56

Phew. yeah things seem 2 have calmed down. but tellin ya he really hounded and interrogated me and I nearly fkin cracked!

29. Mar. 00.29

Thnx – but things a lot better now. I just kept repeating over and over that u and me r just really good friends :) hope Ive convinced him!

29. Mar. 01.01

Hes gone into town. and yes Im 100% sure ur duvet would be an enchanted shield against a wicked world :) gonna get a shower now and a good nights sleep. dream naked dreams my hunk – preferably about me of course! :) kisses all over.

. . .

29. Mar. 10.05

Yeah totally! Amazin he bought that about us being just friends.

29. Mar. 10.37

But u know J that me and Gustav have barely touched each other in over a year. and the thing that really calmed him down was he seriously believes Im actually a closet dyke! :-O so ur out of the firin range babe :) but of course him thinkin I prefer women just makes him more of a joke ffs.

29. Mar. 10.56

Yeah but imagine he can be so off beam and know me so badly. but well leave him 2 his ravings and we can carry on without having 2 worry – yay! :) and now that urge is coming on me 2 let you totally nail me!

29. Mar. 14.02

And now Im so behind schedule its shocking. thought Id better send a greeting and tell u that real life sucks.

29. Mar. 14.47

Sitting here wondering if ur fed up 2 ur back teeth of constant texts from me saying I miss u?

29. Mar. 14.54

Intensely.

29. Mar. 23.26

Aw man! what a day and a half that was! – nite oh wonderful man. Ill be rushing home tomorrow 2 rescue Lærke from a nanny. so if uve time and the inclination :) we can be 2gether on Thursday? the whole day? yay! kisses.

. . .

30. Mar. 12.01

Really need u 2 take a really fkin hard hold of my body babe! am nearly forgetting what it feels like ffs. just totally focused on u inside me.

. . .

31. Mar. 09.22

Hi babe :) sorry. had 2 go in 2 the office – theres an auction on for one of my titles that closes this morning. breaking my neck here 2 get away before lunchtime! kisses – big wet ones!

31. Mar. 21.14

It was wild 2 c u today. just wild and gorgeous and perfect. AWESOME 2 make love 2 verdis requiem. I love, love it when u fuck me and press ur finger deep up my ass. Im gone babe. just out there. Jonah with dat soooooooooo hot body and passionate heart. whoo :)

31. Mar. 22.07

Did u do the sushi and mad men thing like u said u were going 2 do?

31. Mar. 22.26

Yeah it changes its style at the start. what about sushi and cava tomorrow?

31. Mar. 22.35

C u around six :) hope u can sleep all right on those
mucked up sheets :)

. . .

APRIL

1. Apr. 10.00

I can well understand u getting a physical reaction babe
I mean u were fairly fkin vigorous yesterday – whoo! :-O
probably just as well Lærke was there 2 cramp r style a
bit cuz things wud probably have got out of hand :)

1. Apr. 13.06

Delighted ur not squeamish about blood :) blood seems
2 b a feature of our "thing" :) love, love that u adore my
body and everything that stems from that.

1. Apr. 23.01

Shall we meet at Letz Sushi? Im paying :) soooo looking
4ward 2 all these new erotic places ur going 2 bring me
2. even tho ur not physically beside me I feel u so close.
nite nite baby. sleep tite. kisses :)

. . .

2. Apr. 10.46

An avalanche of gorgeous naked thoughts from here J.
just daydreaming of u taking me from behind. my cunt
round, taut, quivering, dilated wet and waiting 4 u :) 4
that moment when u explode in me.

2. Apr. 11.01

Hope u all enjoy brunch :)

2. Apr. 11.31

When ur physically back 2 the top J, think wed be doing
it at least three times a week :) it was sooooo lovely 2 b
by ur side when u woke up.

2. Apr. 17.23

What do u say 2 a marathon sex romp 2morrow day?
have 2 work. tho I kud do it at urs. plus a fuckathon
of course! promise 2 be careful. not 2 many twists +
contortions :)

2. Apr. 23.37

Really fkin annoying reading that article about B in
Politiken today. Im still raging I didnt get that gig. but
u have 2 read it J. its a fantastic book :) did u read
madame bovary in the end? soooooooo dying for
sloooow (careful) sex with u :)

. . .

3. Apr. 18.20

Another waaaay 2 short lunch with u guy! I love, love
when you lick me out. even tho its a bit vlad the impaler
or what? :):) deliriously happy under ur duvet.

3. Apr. 22.48

Fkin weird having 2 leave right then. after such an
intimate conversation. not 2 mention bodies :) wanna
continue tomorrow? exactly where we stopped :) miss u.

3. Apr. 23.53

J have 2 spend whole of 2morrow morning with Lærke at
the creche ffs. so itll b afternoon b4 I show up at urs . . .
shud b in ur bed right now already! :) nite nite hunkster.
loadz of kisses and sorry if Ive knocked ur recovery plan
back a few weeks :-O but ur my strong man with strong
hands :)

. . .

4. Apr. 10.27

Jeez now Im stuck in one of them playschool centres
outside of town with thousands of skreemin brats –
WTF? kids creches and me defo do not mix. waaaaaay
2 many kids :)

4. Apr. 11.42

Lærkes just done a drawing of me – shes calling it
"Pippi-Mum." as in longstocking. nothing like me but
aw . . . lovely thought bless her :)

4. Apr. 20.25

Im literally missing u already ffs. but I admit I got a shock
when next door banged on the wall as we bonked! :):)

4. Apr. 20.35

Anyway kudnt u do massive grunts and groans next time
2 annoy them even more? :)

4. Apr. 21.43

Im thinking coming over 2 u every chance I get. till u
get sick of me :) and start giving me the "long silences"
treatment :)

. . .

5. Apr. 08.14

Was in the middle of answering ur text and fell asleep
with phone in hand – maybe an overdose of fresh air :)

5. Apr. 10.01

Amazing u can make me cum in a way that makes me
just totally disappear – again and again and again.
wonderful and this is when u r recuperating from a major
op?! :-O

5. Apr. 11.38

Breaking my neck 2 get 2 c u b4hand :) have 2 go
out and buy stuff when I get a minute, but what about
tomorrow? how long will u be at the hospital on
Thursday?

5. Apr. 15.22

OMG have u seen my total dream house is for sale in
the property section? shall we buy it J? that would b
fantastic :)

5. Apr. 15.35

Have u seen it? waddya think babe? OMG buy a house together. yeah . . .

5. Apr. 15.37

Married? do u have 2 b married 2 buy a house 2gether?

5. Apr. 15.48

Well totally agree have 2 get divorced first! :)

5. Apr. 16.11

Yeah but when ur musthave dream house goes on sale u get the final piece in the jigsaw guy! :) but its way 2 big 4 just me and Lærke so . . . :)

5. Apr. 16.29

No! we wud buy it cuz it wud be awesome and cozy and lovely and sweet 2 live there with u :)

5. Apr. 21.58

So uve finally watched Trinity :) just ring when u get a chance :) remember we have 2 watch the last episode together! kisses.

5. Apr. 22.36

U r probably the person I keep the least secrets from J – mucho kisses! :) hope we c each other tomorrow!

. . .

6. Apr. 10.58

AWESOME that uve already been 2 the bank 2 discuss house purchases and shit but do u seriously think u kud stand it out in the country? :) Im overloaded with proofing and corrections here. trying 2 concentrate but theres a deep current of yeah Im happy running thru me :)

6. Apr. 11.15

R u a totally happy bunny my man? :) way cool! :) but also a bit worrying seeing as uve been watching murders all nite! :) trying 2 get finished here so I can get home 2 u.

6. Apr. 23.00

No its that reality TV thing I told u about Single Life. the bit where the 22 year old girl says (OMG): mum taught me how 2 give a proper blowjob by getting me 2 practice on 99 cones – ya know ice cream cornets with a flake in them? best way 2 learn how 2 avoid tearing the skin with ur teeth. but hey if Im giving a blowjob it has 2 b superclean as well. I mean if a guy reeks of old cheese down there. ya know what we call cocky cheese? well I just tell him straight and get him 2 wash his meat and 2 veg do u know waddamean? that's b4 I start anything at all man. (joy slides two huge silicone inserts into her bra as she explains 2 her mum how certain types of condom can help with dryness in the vagina but joys mother replies – well my cunts never dry darling) :-O can u c the double edged dysfunction with these 2 losers – thats

what they r. and 2 some extent me 2 4 watching that shit
late in the evening so I dont have 2 think. hey J! dont
take my tongue in cheek texts 2 seriously babe :)

6. Apr. 23.57
Hope u werent too startled at that mad shit :) crazy
about u. millions of so not cheesy kisses :):):)

. . .

7. Apr. 19.29
Soooooooooo want 2 b naked with u. just feel ur soft skin
against mine ffs.

. . .

8. Apr. 13.55
I truly believe that, no matter what happens, not having u
in my life is unthinkable after all weve been thru together.
may b Im saying that cuz Ive not had that many serious
relationships. and dont start reading that as a sign of a
breakup! :)

8. Apr. 14.43
Well get 2 the bottom of something tomorrow! kisses
baby :)

8. Apr. 21.57
Am at Rio Bravo. lotsa peeps here! :) kisses :)

8. Apr. 23.04

Yeah Gustav was appearing but I didnt c much of it cuz I was seeing 2 Lærke mostly. surprises me a bit how much u keep an eye on that scene :)

8. Apr. 23.15

J Im not sure why I try 2 hide the fact I watch Gustav acting. may b I do it more for Lærke's sake?

8. Apr. 23.25

Sorry J really sorry and of course ur totally right. that kind of secrecy is not exactly a good basis for buying a house together :)

. . .

9. Apr. 11.58

Really need 2 kiss you ffs. what if I come over in a bit? crazy for and about u babe :) with or without clothes! :-O

9. Apr. 18.47

Bit fkin sad and boring we cant kiss when and wherever we want. even more pathetic we wont c each other now till the end of next week :(

9. Apr. 19.02

OK u already say we shud b able 2 kiss where we want but ur not the one with a kid 2 protect.

9. Apr. 22.53

Think Im actually a bit jealous ur at a party that one of ur exes is also at . . . am I being weird or what?

10. Apr. 00.19

OK that was probably out of order but all the same . . . and yes Im still living with Gustav. so thnx 4 the text – hope ur enjoying urself.

. . .

10. Apr. 19.09

Arrived in London baby and now enjoying a glass of wine in a park. its warm and lovely here. how did things work with ur ex from Hellerup?

10. Apr. 19.20

Yes I know Ive said previously I dont get jealous, but Im obviously not a consistent person. just the way I am Im afraid!

10. Apr. 21.22

Of course its good u still talk like civil human beings – know Im being a pain here and have no right 2 interrogate u about ur life :)

11. Apr. 00.04

Well maybe Im jealous because Im quite insecure about u.

. . .

11. Apr. 09.10

Gr8 2 talk properly today J – no. not insecure anymore :)

11. Apr. 13.54

Loadz of positive and productive meetings here – but
miss u.

11. Apr. 14.46

Or just say fuck it and have a smoochfest right in the
middle of the bookfair :-O

11. Apr. 14.55

Yeah I mean totally open – no more ducking and diving
– fuck it J!

11. Apr. 15.12

Soooo want 2 feel my hand down ur pants and round ur
cock! actually right in there right now having really horny
on fire sex with u – if u were here :)

11. Apr. 22.53

Jesus anxiety attack doesnt sound good J. so r u really
down babe? hope not. be back soon remember. kisses :)

11. Apr. 23.42

U cant just push me away like that J! cuz I don't want 2 b
just the distant friend.

11. Apr. 23.55

Well u kud help me when Im insecure instead of going
on about how distant I am ffs.

12. Apr. 00.26

WTF? What dyu mean u dont trust me?

12. Apr. 00.53

Yes I trust u. but its still fkin weird 4 me if u go 2 a party
with an ex! plus like Ive said Im not totes sure whether ur
just sick of waiting 4 me or not. like I soooo know that u
kud get someone a lot less problematic and better yeah?

12. Apr. 01.10

Thanks J. I know I know. dont know why I have 2 b
reassured all the time ffs :(:-O :)

. . .

12. Apr. 08.33

Sorry J fell asleep and have just seen ur text now. no I
dont mean 2 b stirring shit 4 no good reason. sry babe.
I know its only me u want and of course u cant just give
up ur old friends while ur waiting around 4 me 2 sort
things. really sorry that all this makes me behave like a
nutcracker. I AM trying 2 b better. hope all goes well at
the hospital and ur checkups.

12. Apr. 10.34

4got 2 say really miss u and ur loving kisses.

12. Apr. 12.25

Thnx J and same 2 u. end of wistful pining texts from here when u don't even bother 2 answer them :) but will u at least let me know straight away when u get ur hospital results?

12. Apr. 23.39

Just arrived at very swanky party. will u still be up in half an hour?

13. Apr. 03.21

Finally back at base. hope you get a gr8 sleep baby.

. . .

13. Apr. 16.02

Jeez above. totally wrecked tired. but last meeting shortly and then I just wanna get home.

13. Apr. 16.17

That really dozn't sound good about Jeppe's partner. I didnt know they did that with spontaneous miscarriages. thats the best thing about clinical abortions – the whole things over there and then. hope Jeppe looks after her now. tuff few weeks ahead. Im sure he will. kisses.

13. Apr. 16.50

Whoah where did that come from? of course surgical abortions are over very quickly J. thats the whole point no? how far on was she remind me?

13. Apr. 17.13
Let me know when its all over. r u at the hospital right now?

. . .

14. Apr. 10.48
Do u want 2 c me anytime soon?

14. Apr. 11.02
I miss u like mad J but am worried ur backing out on me.

14. Apr. 11.45
Ud b very welcome 2 reply telling me whether ur backing out of "us"!?

14. Apr. 12.28
Sorry J. of course ur worried about Jeppe and Sara. but really need 2 c u, like, fairly soon? . . . Im as horny as fuck guy! what if I c if I can leave work early?

14. Apr. 13.39
Fkin mad 2 kiss u all over! long long loooooong ones and up close and very personal. just have 2 pick up Lærke first. reckon I can leave here in just over an hour :)

14. Apr. 14.29
Just have 2 bid half a million on a book – like u do :) fairly sure I can leave right after :)

14. Apr. 18.02

Have really urgent need 2 have sex with u again. sorry
if I was a bit weird with u today. kind of felt u were
gonna tell me u just kudnt b bothered anymore. but
honestly . . . Im so mad about u and I know its me
making things complicated when theres really no need.

14. Apr. 19.37

Noh! the crush is still there and wants 2 stay :) soooo
longing for a load of nights in ur bed. after raunchy sex
and torrents of hot kisses.

14. Apr. 23.23

Me and Lærke fell asleep together :) just have 2 sort
a few things here and back 2 dreamland :) maybe we
could eat together tomorrow?

. . .

15. Apr. 09.34

Say hello 2 Jeppe from me and tell him that this time
next year his partner will be sitting feeding a baby.

15. Apr. 13.06

We can eat at mine as long as it doesnt feel 2 weird 4 u?
what do u think?

15. Apr. 13.22

Have 2 go back into town 2 buy a present after Ive
collected Lærke :) so not sure I can manage it . . . r Sara
and Jeppe OK?

15. Apr. 13.35

Yay that wud b gr8! :):) well get over 2 u asap – such a
relief u like little Lærke – big hello 2 Sara and Jeppe!

15. Apr. 14.04

OMG – just bid half mill on a book J – shivers or what!!

15. Apr. 22.10

What a really brilliant and entertaining evening. cant
believe Lærke peed all over ur chair and floor – really
sorry J! :) think u handled it very well and reassuringly
:) Ill get the spare underwear u gave us back 2 u soon –
very useful but bit on the large side! hope the pictures u
took of us with ur fancy camera come out well.

15. Apr. 23.54

All tied up and gift wrapped – special delivery just 4 u.

16. Apr. 00.11

My whole body is quivering and on a high – getting
ready 2 surrender myself 2 u :)

. . .

16. Apr. 10.10

Did u get 2 c Hank Moody? Thnx 4 yesterday. when I
think of what u do 2 my body I actually go red and get a
flush of wet – time after time.

16. Apr. 11.00

Its both awesome and very unpleasant going round in
drenched panties!

16. Apr. 11.16

Have 2 say it right out J. NEED U 2 FUCK ME RIGHT
NOW :-O loooooooooongg and thrusting and way out
there beyond the edge of the world.

16. Apr. 11.56

Cant stop wishing u were biting and nipping at my tits
and nipples. licking my wet pussy out. slinging me over
on the bed. holding me down really roughly. tying me up
and taking me till I feel u coming like an express train.
me pinioned as u shoot up me in me.

16. Apr. 14.07

Totally J. lets go 4 it and do it. want u 2 take me 2
unknown places. Im game 4 anything and everything –
my body is urs. sitting in the train now trying 2 focus on
something other than ur massive cock in my mouth.

. . .

17. Apr. 16.26

Gr8 buzz at the party here in V. :) getting the train so Ill
be in around 10pm. Ill text when Im not far off.

. . .

18. Apr. 13.04

Magical again guy! :-O longing 4 u rite this sec. again.
wasnt easy 2 leave ur pit this morning I tell ya. just
wanted more duvet time! whats the plan 4 tonite?

18. Apr. 14.57

Im a full of the sex joys of spring right now and really
wud try fkin anything :):):) – WHOA – was a bit thrown
there as we were talking – who pops his head in the
door but the one and only Jørgen Lett – whoohoo
megastar time!

18. Apr. 18.16

Namedropper? WTF? :) ffs J u know all of them better
than me! b there in about a quarter of an hour. just
waiting 4 a wash 2 finish :)

. . .

19. Apr. 09.57

Had a gorgeous sleep – safe and cozy by ur side last
night baby! but fuck – Lærke and Gustav r due back very
soon. this evening even. not sure what time. Ill rush over
2 u after work but have 2 go 2 the house first for five
mins :)

19. Apr. 10.40

Sorry J. forgot u had 2 do that. gimme a buzz when ur done out there.

19. Apr. 11.23

Totally salacious erotic and kinda taboo breaking u taking all those pictures of my pussy yesterday – Ive never let anyone do anything like that b4 :-O hope theyre better than that pussybox stuff on the net. watabout u taking pictures of me as u fuck me from behind next time we do it? Ive never seen that :) u push out my boundaries the whole time. kisses.

. . .

19. Apr. 20.14

Didnt get that senior editor's job after all J ffs – a so called colleague snatched it from right under my nose – its really not funny anymore :(

19. Apr. 20.30

Yeah they had basically promised it was mine and Ive worked my tits off 2 get it – very fkin hard 2 take. biting my tongue here!

20. Apr. 02.30

Fuck major crisis here at home as well. Im a total wreck with it. WTF am I going 2 do with Gustav?

. . .

21. Apr. 20.04

J. Im scared stiff of losing u. I know its not same 4 u but
I think life would be impossible if I lost u – have just read
a load of old messages from u. feel close 2 u now and
Ive got this gorgeous warm tingle running thru me.

. . .

22. Apr. 17.05

It's really shitty how u always go quiet when I mention
the words trouble or crisis! and I know ur just going 2
say – well just move in with me – but things just aint
that simple :) where exactly r u rite now I wonder? really
thinking about u a lot.

22. Apr. 20.07

I think Im probably OK. but just wrecked with all dis
emotional self torturing shit and worrying I put myself
thru. have just read a novel with yet another main female
character that resembles me waaaaaaaay too much!
on the plus side all this sunshine has given me lots of
beautiful new freckles.

. . .

23. Apr. 10.35

Have u seen Politiken today? that first book I bought
in and edited was given 5 stars!! but tbh its no surprise
that something that basically arose from romps in ur bed
gets a megawriteup :)

. . .

24. Apr. 20.05
When do u get back?

24. Apr. 21.44
OK. thnx. take care

. . .

25. Apr. 15.17
My dear gorgeous hunk of a man. its been a really
stressful Easter. nothings become simpler in any way.
but one thing I do know is I still really want 2 c u. thats if
u still want 2 c me of course? or r there other babes on
their way 2 ur bed even as we speak?

25. Apr. 15.27
Now dont get ur blood boiling like that. it cant be good
for ur heart J.

25. Apr. 16.09
What I mean is that I used the Easter break 2 get a bit of
badly needed order in my life. like Ive said b4 countless
times Im NOT dumping all my chaos on u but then failing
2 commit. but 4 the time being at least it just seems 2
easy 2 walk away from everything. Ive got a young child
2 consider dont 4get. like, 2 give up we have 2 b able 2
say we tried everything. and me and Gustav defo havnt

done that yet. even tho theres been no physical contact
4 over a year. of course Ill understand if u decide its not
worth it 4 u. its not a gr8 situation I admit.

25. Apr. 16.25

No J u really havent been given the red card honestly.
theres nothing more I want 2 do in life than keep seeing
u. ur well aware of that. but Im just saying how things
stand and that I can understand if u lose patience with
me.

25. Apr. 16.55

At the risk of u thinking Im a total coward and neurotic,
its my child Ive prioritized as I keep saying. I just couldn't
justify ruining her world. I think I wud disintegrate if I had
that on my conscience.

25. Apr. 17.15

J! no Im not fkin slinking off with my tail between my legs
as u put it! u know that very fkin well and also that I DO
actually dare 2 say all these things straight 2 ur face.
and I am in no way going cold on u. I feel the same as I
did when I first saw u over a year ago. and I feel like shit
by the way. really shit and terrible and torn and u dont
seem 2 have any fkin sympathy 4 my position?

25. Apr. 17.44

Hypocrite? hypocrite? how dare u call me that!? cant
believe ur being so fkin aggressive with me.

25. Apr. 17.55

What exactly is it Ive done today that was so awful 2 make u go on about me like that? fact is the only thing I really want 2 do is kiss u but thats obviously something Im going 2 have 2 get over in future.

25. Apr. 18.04

:):)

25. Apr. 18.08

Was thinking of coming over later?

25. Apr. 18.23

Have 2 sort some boring things first – round half past nine, tennish? but if ur still raging with me I dont think I kud handle it tbh . . . ?

. . .

26. Apr. 09.12

Back here. Heading into an atrocious week. Really longing 4 u and more time off ffs. hot kisses baby :)

26. Apr. 10.03

Just read our texts from yesterday. OMG :-O phew! uha :) hope u have a gr8 day.

26. Apr. 10.39

Kisses, thousands of kisses just 4 u :):)

26. Apr. 10.44

I can just c u going round in ur bathrobe and drinking a smoothie. dying 2 b in ur bed big boy . . . that is all!

26. Apr. 11.57

Im fairly sure I know what it was that annoyed u in r text fight the other day – so I totally agree with ur delete b4 u bitch formula. think we should try really hard 2 just be happy and celebrate "us" when we r 2gether. its dumb 2 fight and quarrel when weve so little time with each other. of course I want 2 talk 2 u about serious and important things, but in a constructive way. I respect u far 2 much 2 get caught up in a mess of idiotic utterances!

26. Apr. 13.06

Im so lucky Ive met u J. Ive told u this b4 but regardless of what happens in the future I just cant imagine u not being in my life.

26. Apr. 13.20

I just cant imagine u not being in my life :)

26. Apr. 23.45

When I was putting Lærke 2 bd she talked 4 ages about the scar on ur arm and turned it into a kind of story. uve really made a big impression on her. sleep good baby :) kisses upon kisses :)

. . .

27. Apr. 10.00

Morning baby. already sick 2 death of the drama queens here at work. believe me enjoy and appreciate yet another day of peace and tranquillity at home b4 u have 2 get back that sort of crap :) kisses

27. Apr. 11.13

And may I take a little bit of the credit 4 u still being such an incredible lover? :) gr8 2 hear ur making such good progress. will try very best 2 get away early 2morrow. kisses.

27. Apr. 23.29

Will hopefully b b4 :) Ill let u know :) nite nite baby. sleep tite. kisses

. . .

28. Apr. 15.51

C u at 5.

29. Apr. 00.20

Its just so brilliant and gorgeous 2 b with u J and of course thats also what makes things so hard. when I dont c u for a few days I really miss ur company and chat. nite nite. :) sweet dreams – about me! :) we have 2 do a lot more talking. its gr8 :)

. . .

29. Apr. 10.17

Do u have 2 go 2 the hospital today as well J? kisses :)

. . .

30. Apr. 10.34

What about tomorrow? think Im very fuckable again . . .

. . .

MAY

1. May 12.01
Maybe we kud meet around 2 in the park – Id like 2 hear more about Jeppe + S. otherwise c u at 4.

1. May 20.57
I know it was my own fault I had 2 leave. but even after a few minutes of being away from u I get the shakes 4 u – just mad 2 b back in ur arms again. totally entwined around ur body under the canopy of stars twinkling thru ur bedroom window!

1. May 22.26
I always feel like a gap suddenly emerges in my life. as if Im missing a body part as soon as I leave u. but then I focus on the fact were going 2 c each other again very soon. and that ur physically not very far away :) then u feel really close 2 me again. can still feel ur kisses on my lips.

1. May 23.14
U have really penetrated deep under my skin and bones J. sleep good my darling hunk :) kisses.

. . .

2. May 10.56

Welcome back 2 work babe! :) love, love u r just a few buildings away from me.

2. May 17.10

Yeah I know. Im the same. weird feeling trying 2 act normal when others talk about u :) soooooooo gorgeous with u yesterday :)

2. May 21.39

Mad 2 fuck u right now this second ffs. feel ur skin and hear those noises u make when u touch me OMG. when were 2gether u leave something deep inside me that makes me long 2 get back 2 ur bed. fantastic and frustrating in one and the same big dipper ride! :)

. . .

3. May 15.05

Managed 2 extricate myself from this evenings meeting – should I come over?

3. May 15.50

OK thats fine. Ill get Lærke early instead then. enjoy the evening!

3. May 15.55

No J really. Not peeved in the least :) say hello 2 Jeppe.

3. May 16.04

Ah shit now I think of it. had a gr8 alibi 2 stay out till very l8. had planned some fantastic sex games in ur bed :-O so now u know what ur missing guy! kisses from ur ever faithful mistress :)

3. May 16.20

Yeah but I need 2 feel u exploding inside me very urgently. not 2 much 2 ask :)

3. May 20.11

R we really going 2 c each other tomorrow? whoohoo :) and next Thursday I think I can stay all night with u.

3. May 21.40

Fuck. How Id love 2 bomb over 2 urs and wrap myself round u. already dying 2 get hammered and nailed by u again.

3. May 22.11

Were gonna have 2 really fuck each other up and down all over the place. I mean not just in ur bed. just wherever we want. whatever space. I love, love it when u grip my ass so tight it makes me gasp and ram it up me then lick me out till I arch backwards and come over and over again.

3. May 22.29

My body has been on pins the whole day. as if my nerves r all exposed and screaming 4 ur hands.

. . .

4. May 11.38

Yeah were crazy busy here ffs. totally under siege again 2day. when do u think ull get home?

4. May 11.50

Soooo look 4ward 2 seeing u around 4.

4. May 13.14

Sooooooo sorry babe but have 2 cancel our rv. things falling apart at home and Ive pains all over. especially in my stomach. can divorce provoke physical pains? bit of a mess and annoying but I dont think I wud be good company today.

4. May 15.48

Thnx 4 that J. yeah I feel really shit. like Im gonna have a breakdown or something. really looking 4ward 2 seeing u. if I need 2 get away all of a sudden wud be really gr8 if I knew whether ur home?

4. May 16.01

Need 2 b hugged by u sooooo much. Ill text b4 I appear at ur door.

. . .

5. May 10.51

Just feel all broken. As if Id been knocked down by a truck. do u have time and desire 2 c me 2day? kisses :)

5. May 11.45

At the hospital? had totally forgotten!

5. May 15.18

So around 4pm?

5. May 15.32

Cant fkin wait :)

5. May 20.34

Was just so wild and gorgeous 2 make love with u 2day. Im just one big erogenous zone in ur hands.

5. May 21.44

Have a huge and continual need 2 b with u. always seems like I have 2 leave at the very point when Im so loving being in ur arms. just say if u get fed up w/ me.

. . .

6. May 09.11

Thot I kud feel ur cum from yesterday dripping out of me when I biked 2 work this morning. made me a bit heady and horny. do I have a screw loose do u think? :-O :)

6. May 11.58

OK Ill come over just after that then.

6. May 11.58

Ill probably land in a bit of a drunken state and wearing stilettos.

6. May 13.09

Have 2 show my face at a little birthday party first :)

6. May 13.42

I normally leave early at her parties anyway cuz she lets people smoke indoors – cant bear it 4 long. shes from H. everybody smokes everywhere there. even at the dinner table. yuk.

6. May 13.55

Brilliant :) ur most welcome 2 come and rescue me. need 2 b rescued, carried off and violently fucked.

6. May 21.23

My dear gorgeous hunk :) my parents were thrilled with that lovely photo u took of Lærke. in fact they took it home with them. mega compliment 2 u.

. . .

8. May 12.15

Whoo! that final orgasm u gave me yesterday was just

out there. its still rippling in my body. kisses :) thinking of
u constantly.

8. May 12.25
This morning as I lay in ur arms I dreamt I was walking
round bare footed, wearing a long flowing shift so fine
it was see thru and me big bellied carrying ur baby. the
sun was all bright and shiny – we were in a large villa
facing right onto a beach.

8. May 12.35
Sure it was a dream – but with you dreams often turn 2
reality :)

8. May 12.45
Shit babe. that sounds quite serious?

8. May 12.53
Want 2 meet at urs?

8. May 13.02
OK. on the way. with nothing tagging along :)

. . .

9. May 14.35
Have 2 buy curtains at ikea tomorrow. kisses :) as for
yesterday – what u did! – ur sex slave.

9. May 15.53

Did I ever tell u that Im madly in love with u?

9. May 22.02

That's really good of u J :) but Ive hired a car. whats ur day like 2morrow?

. . .

10. May 17.41

It will be late. at least 10pm. that OK? or do u need ur beauty sleep?

. . .

11. May 19.19

Ikea is always gr8 fun! can b at urs at eight thirty.

. . .

12. May 10.13

It was magical and delicious – me and u last night – ahhhh . . .

12. May 13.35

J. when u come 2 this little get together at our house, its EXTREMELY important 2 remember u r TOTALLY unaware that Im taking over Mia's portfolio AND that u dont know a THING about me or my work. u just kind of know me vaguely :)

12. May 18.07

Just got home. can we just get a delivery or somethin and eat in? bit down :(there in 20.

. . .

13. May 11.09

Sorry I was a bit flat last night J. havent a clue why. I love being with u. maybe thats actually what makes the whole thing more difficult. maybe the 2 of us are massively emotional in our own complicated ways?

13. May 11.42

How r u? I keep getting weird feelings. maybe Im going down with some heavy bug ffs.

13. May 13.31

We have loadz of awkward feelings and vibes going on between us J. purely physically as well. my body still aches all over. all of a sudden that song love hurts makes sense. maybe we shud time out for a few days so we can each work out what we shud do with these feelings? the point of "our thing" was never 2 make each other feel sad or down.

13. May 13.55

Making love with u is like a dream thats actually happening. magical when ur deep inside me. close as skin 2 each other.

13. May 14.01

Last night I kud feel ur not sure about me. think that's
why I feel so crap and in pain.

13. May 15.08

Hope ur not gonna do one of those numbers where u
get me 2 say its over so I then am not quite so down cuz
u dont want this any more?

13. May 18.33

Thnx for those beautiful words J. of course I can feel
ur doubt about whether Im really serious about having
a relationship with u. Im well aware u have deep love
4 me and u really need 2 know that I dont want 2 just
disappear out of ur life . . .

. . .

16. May 14.22

Hope uve had a good and thoughtful weekend?

16. May 14.57

Sounds gr8! Looking 4ward 2 reading D's book. Ive just
received it.

16. May 15.14

OMG did u c the queen J? . . . everytime I see her Im
just, like, starstruck. Camilla was there 2 wasnt she?
standing very close 2 her. she said it was unreal.

16. May 15.47

Yeah shes both fascinating and super cool. sorry but Ive lent that 2 someone else. T is good. read a lot of hers at uni. do u think Im namedropping again? :):):)

. . .

17. May 15.19

Everything OK?

. . .

18. May 11.08

Did u leave right after ur meeting here J? Are we seeing each other later?

18. May 11.30

Really missing u babe!

18. May 11.59

OK! :) officially we dont know each other but the fact is u probably know me much better than anyone else :) why arent u answering my q about seeing each other? dont u want 2?

18. May 13.01

Sorry J but uve just been really quiet of late – didnt mean 2 get u all worked up babe.

. . .

19. May 20.20

What a fkin day guy! several looooooong hours on my
own with 2 very clever and pedantic lawyers. but do u
know what? I actually handled them surprisingly well :)
kisses :)

. . .

20. May 16.42

Whats with these long silences ffs? maybe its best 2
cancel tomorrow? assume u agree?

20. May 19.39

Think Im running a temperature – fell asleep and didnt
hear phone ring. everything gets 10 x harder when r
misunderstandings run us off the rails. do u not think we
shud meet up J?

20. May 19.59

Yes. lets talk babe. what about 2morrow at 2-ish at urs?

20. May 20.39

Soooooooooooo looking 4ward 2 seeing u baby!

. . .

21. May 09.18

Gone down bad with something today J. kudnt cope with meeting up today. really sorry :(

21. May 18.02

So deliriously happy with ur text J. I honestly dont think uve put me thru more than Ive put u thru. we r just, like, knife-edge out there on a highwire thing – magically exciting and fantastically difficult. kud do with a few soothing kisses on my forehead – and a lot of other places . . .

22. May 00.04

Whoah – my bodys suddenly longing 2 b abused again! :)

. . .

22. May 14.34

Im a lot better – but the nausea just wont go away. reading scripts here which are unfortunately quite good. so Im gonna have 2 make decisions about them and do writeups. what ur plans? kisses :)

22. May 16.25

Well excuse me! Spanish Latino reception. my my! do u still c a lot of whatshername? that translator? got a feeling this nausea is leaving me but still only want toast and butter. and u of course.

22. May 18.08

Wud really appreciate it if u wud let me know if ur still seeing other wimmin :)

22. May. 19.15

Thnx ur making me a lot happier. really great ur back in circulation and Ill b even happier when u tell me Im still ur one and only. kisses :)

. . .

23. May 11.08

Was the reception a blast? Going 2 c a play today with Petra. are we seeing each other tomorrow J?

. . .

24. May 21.21

Sex with u at least 3 times a week wud b exquisite.

. . .

25. May 10.59

Dear hunk of hunks :) really lovely 2 c u last night. fkin nuts about u. soooooooo gorgeous knowing ur up and about and very near me :)

. . .

26. May 16.40

Yeah! hard physical training really rocks doesnt it. :)
Whew! super busy at work 2day. had a really fascinating
chat with Petra. sitting alone reading in a cafe right now.
ur going for a meal tonight arent u babe?

27. May 20.55

Remember 2 watch urself. dont think its a good idea
ur back working such long hours already. were seeing
each other sometime soon arent we? what ur plans 4 da
weekend?

27. May 23.44

Nite nite sleep tite baby :) hard 2 fall asleep knowing ur
probably lying naked not very far from me!

. . .

28. May 20.52

Me and Lærke going 2 kids play at 1pm. Have dire need
of hot orgasms around 3-ish. OK?

. . .

29. May 18.35

4got my sunglasses and panties again ffs – think also I
left myself there at urs. Ill just nip over at half past 8. is
that OK?

. . .

30. May 20.05

Missing u massively at the moment J :-O

. . .

31. May 09.23

Fell asleep with Lærke but have felt really UP all day :)
love 2 think of us 2 2gether. with or without clothes. have
u time 4 coffee 2day?

31. May 10.30

After work? what time u going home? Im picking Lærke
up just after four. wanna meet at our special cafe?

31. May 15.03

I registered as a blood donor a while back but have 2 get
a test now. have 2 sign this form saying Ive not engaged
in "potentially unsafe sexual behaviour" in the last six
months. so this is where u come in . . . assuming uve
been checked 4 everything. haven't u?

31. May 15.53

Thought as much :) Im probably iron deficient. and J
deficient!

31. May 20.54

Shes fast asleep and Im more or less awake :) so come
over asap guy!

31. May 21.05

No. Im absolutely not 2 tired 2 c u :) but its pouring rain out there . . .

31. May 21.10

Love, love that umbrella of urs. c u soon babe :):):)

. . .

JUNE

1. June 00.47

Its really fkin hard when u go – I just love us being
2gether so much and yeah OK not a particularly nice
feeling that its my fault things are so complicated! kisses
:) gonna close my eyes now and just dream of making
love with u.

. . .

1. June 17.23

So basically Ive done nothing but think about sex
with u the whole day and in every way, position and
permutation possible! :-O – like I told u Im here visiting
my parents for the next few days. gonna be hard doing
without u.

. . .

2. June 12.20

Fuck just stubbed my toe hard on one of the thousands
of stone curbs my folks have laid out in the pathways
round their grounds. talk about fkin crazy paving man.
think Im gonna lose the nail ffs – totally not funny :(
kisses over all of naked u.

. . .

3. June 12.19

Hey gorgeous hunk! down at the beach here with Lærke. really lovely beach :) but my debit card must have been stolen when we were at the station waiting for the train yesterday. only noticed it now. a bit down and shocked tbh :(have worked out I dont do being alone. wud b gr8 if u were here on the beach with us :) really missing u babe.

3. June 15.06

Yeah just my debit card but they managed 2 use over a thousand before I got it blocked – fuckers. still kudda been a LOT worse.

3. June 15.55

Thnx babe :) steamy hot kisses from ur lips r da best help of all! and yes reported it 2 cops and all seems sorted now.

3. June 16.20

No never heard of William Sidis? wud like 2 borrow it if its good. reading Murakami and old Greek myths today. had 2 read something a bit more highbrow after d. p. – it actually is really beautiful here.

. . .

5. June 13.26

Time has just flown by. long weekend tho next week thank god. them fkin thieving lowlives still annoying me.

5. June 15.07

Actually stayed at my folks till yesterday – then went straight 2 insane party with Petra and a few others from work. nursing a wicked hangover now. wud now very much like 2 do pleasurable penance 4 missed (bonking! :)) time with u in the coming weeks – if u want that is?

5. June 17.28

OK being with u is not a penance ffs :) stop being difficult and hard 2 please J :):):):) u know what I mean guy!

5. June 17.35

Ur too easily pleased? awhh – now I feel bad :) soooooooo looking 4ward 2 seeing u baby! Im like nuts nuts nuts :)

. . .

6. June 21.31

Hi J. not heard much from u baby :) really hope u still want 2 c me tomorrow? at urs yes?

. . .

8. June 11.10

Hi hunk of hunks :) no not at all. uve not totally wrecked my body. tho it was close :) am always high as a kite after being with u. who wants 2 sleep when u can get nailed like that :-O kisses

8. June 12.59

Im floating. last night was just fkin awesome. hot.
raunchy. wild and wonderful :)

8. June 20.55

No lie. Im fking crazy about u :)

. . .

9. June 09.32

Morning wonderful man. yeah fell asleep with Lærke.
really deep and with candles still lit ffs – and Gustav
didnt get back till dawn from some party.

9. June 09.33

Meant 2 text u that Im really madly in love with u b4 I fell
asleep. I know its not the same as a beautiful card in the
post but u know . . .

9. June 13.10

Interesting u were turned on reading The Halls 2 people.
Its sposed 2 b the Danish 50 Shades. but quite a few
saying nothing happens. I mean, like, nothing? anyway
u know I love going 2 erotic readings. so raging I wasn't
there. our own kissing 2 b cont. :)

9. June 16.13

5 pm at Joe and the Juice? the one right opposite the
lakes. Ill be in the back part. I like it at the back :)

9. June 20.31

Thnx a mill for ur letter babe – made me all soft, warm and gooey.

9. June 21.14

Even when Im tired, cranky and defo not my charming best? :)

9. June 22.08

Yeah today was very much a day for mega TLC and selfpampering – sometimes I feel like a maimed and battered bird. and that calls 4 serious comfort. gr8 that it doesnt annoy u much. thnx 4 smoothie and also 4 reading that Spanish script! feel free 2 dream about me :) ur gonna have 2 tell me who else u fantasize about sooner or later! nite nite sleep tite baby.

. . .

11. June 10.05

Say what? ur going 2 Spain! why?

11. June 10.13

Eight convalescence days in lovely warm Espana sounds like an excellent idea. itll do u a world of good and its just what u need J. wish I kud go with u – sigh! – but then ud get no rest :):) when do u head off?

11. June 10.20

Jeez the 17th? thats like almost tomorrow – phew! Ill miss u soooooooooo much.

. . .

12. June 11.49

Things completely mental here. lot of stuff whirling round me right now! hope ur OK? got a text from u last night . . . did u get the ones I sent 2 u?

12. June 13.09

Is that all? no there were others ffs. not nice thinking they might b floating round somewhere in cyberspace – like who wants their private texts just suddenly appearing in random places elsewhere :-O

12. June 22.54

Shit didnt realize it was so late. everythings gone into overdrive! missing u madly terribly. have 2 do prep with Petra most of tomorrow, and have a stack of scripts waiting 4 me after that. what u doing Tuesday?

. . .

13. June 11.30

Ive thought long and hard about how I should answer u babe and the only thing I can come up with is – soooooooooo sorry. Im really sorry u feel uve been pushed 2 the back of my 2 do list as u put it. but Im still glad u can see the bigger picture – that this is just one of those phases.

13. June 11.44

Ah come on J. u know very well Im really fond of u and respect u enormously. but I decided 2 spend the weekend thinking a lot of things thru and just closed myself in. it was just Lærke and me. still feel a bit like a maimed and mangled bird and 2 b totally honest havnt a clue what 2 do about it.

13. June 12.01

Whaaaaaat? NEVER. never wud I totally ignore u. wudnt b able 2 babe. never in a million years!

13. June 12.12

So u dont want 6 weeks wondering if ur still my hunk or uve been junked cuz we cant c each other in July? Hello!? its u that's going 2 sunny Spain 4 a break remember? in like three days time? when u know I cant go with u. but that still leaves a lot of June when we can c loadz of each other ffs. but do I take from all this that uve had enuff of "us"?

13. June 12.26

Look. Im fully aware that ur in love with me. but the whole things v complicated. and yes its true I feel guilty where Lærke is concerned. I was almost a child myself when I had her and feel like my youth was just like swallowed up by a crying baby, vomit, nappies and pacifiers and then what about my career?

13. June 12.35

Yes I know. well Im sorry but I just have 2 focus on making sure Lærke has the best I can offer in every way. that of course restricts my own room 4 maneuver – J darling. I really mean it when I say the whole thing upsets me deeply. cuz I can c exactly where ur coming from and how u must feel about it all.

13. June 12.43

I know uve said a thousand times I can just move in with u ffs. but that drives me nuts as well. I mean I really dont think Im good 4 anyone. and maybe especially not 4 ur heart!!

13. June 13.16

OK OK Im flaky then. but its simply not true I dont feel "deeply" enough about us. Ive said loadz of times that its massively frustrating we cant c more of each other than we do. its a rotten place 4 me 2 b in as well dont 4get. and every time I try 2 change things I suddenly start seeing things from Lærkes perspective and I just dont think I can do that 2 her. I know its really cowardly of me but I have 2 go that way . . . but then I feel like a heap of shit about it.

13. June 18.20

Been working with Petra the whole afternoon – hence the late reply. yes J I was a bit miffed at what u wrote cuz its hard 2 think straight where ur concerned. especially when I cant even think straight about myself ffs. but its gr8 we can c each other as soon as u get back from Spain.

13. June 20.43

I think it's a bit 2 easy 4 u 2 put most of the responsibility on my shoulders. me and Lærke move in with u? yeah sure. but Jonah. I really think u kudnt handle the full consequences of that. ur life would b turned upside down with kids and all the restrictions that come with them! but I agree that Ive absolutely no free time at the minute cuz of job and career etc.

13. June 22.01

Sorry J. I was probably a bit hasty earlier on – I do actually think u kud handle us moving in and all that implies. but no. theres not much chance of us seeing each other over the Whitsuntide break. Ive seen u as much as I kud in fairness. sounds gr8 u have all those invites from people over the summer but it really pains me ur so upset about us not being able 2 c each other. but I just cant and its best 2 b clear about it. Ive already made plans for Lærke and Ill b gone most of the summer basically. on top of that Ive had 2 factor in a week of work with Petra 2 plan 4 the autumn script schedule. things r a bit up in the air here at the mo.

13. June 22.24

OK u dont feel particularly appreciated and r annoyed
cuz Ive not consulted u about my holiday plans. all I can
say is my life is not as straightforward as urs – I have a
young child J. u dont. full stop.

14. June 00.04

Yes its true that all our millions of texts over many
months are clear proof of a big love and attraction. so
yeah ur analysis is totally correct. but like I have 2 keep
saying. seen from my life things are unfortunately not
quite as simple as from urs. if u cant grasp that basic
fact weve absolutely no chance of moving on from here.

14. June 00.09

Hope u got that I meant moving on in terms of our
discussion – nothing else :)

14. June 00.21

A few times yesterday u gave big hints that "us" is over.
but just b clear that Ive never at any point said anything
like that. so wudnt mind knowing if its actually u that
wants 2 stop now?

14. June 00.27

Sry babe. was a bit hasty again ffs :) yeah ur right that
uve put a lot of effort into cementing our relationship.
kisses. have 2 sleep now. exhausted. but tomorrow
when u get home from work?

14. June 00.40

OK nite nite sleep tite hon :)

. . .

15. June 09.05

Im really really down babe. cuz I think were fantastic
together. ur 4ever in my thoughts. and remember I
havent disappeared. not in the least. Im still Johanne. Im
still here. and I still kud not envisage u not being in my
life at any point. no way

15. June 09.15

No. I kud never envisage u not being a part of my life.

15. June 15.16

Did u get my text?

15. June 17.26

Am I being frozen out or what?

15. June 17.35

Of course I can understand ur in bits right now and I feel
like Ive been battered then run over by a bus. but like Ive
said b4 love hurts babe.

15. June 18.23

Awrrhh J Im so happy 2 hear u say that. yeah fkin big
time. we shud defo keep seeing each other :)

15. June 18.31

No. I just got the impression u might start calling ur
"rebound" old flames in. how was I 2 know backup
means nurses + doctors doing aftercare on ur heart?
uve said b4 that uve other women lined up.

15. June 21.04

Woha. No J. I know u wud never treat me like that cuz u
really are fking fantastic. Ive told u that so many times.
and I certainly cant be ur nurse. that wud b impossible.
so delighted ur being looked after and that u think we
shud continue our "us" thing. that said I think we shud
really think hard about exactly what we r gonna do yeah?
both right now and going 4ward. were obviously two
very sensitive people who r insanely in love with each
other. but I think we really have 2 think hard instead of
just letting our feelings decide things. but always keep in
mind that I want 2 hear from u wherever and whenever u
feel like. jesus all this is fkin difficult guy!

15. June 21.35

Right then. and if we r going 2 b absolutely clear in r
minds it might b a good idea 2 knock the texting on
the head while ur in Spain a week? 2 get everything
clarified? :)

15. June 22.05

OK it's a deal. But now I feel so miserable and like shit.

. . .

16. June 20.32

Dear gorgeous man. Ive been sitting alone here and
have had loadz of time 2 think. its gonna be a horrible
week without seeing each other and no communication.
It already feels like Im missing a body part or something.
fkin totally weird this.

16. June 20.55

That smiley u sent looks like Mr Angry. is that what it is?

16. June 20.57

Getting loadz of little yellow faces on my phone but
theyre difficult 2 make out. the second one u sent looks
a bit friendlier :)

16. June 21.02

8 ♥ – the girls in PR all got iphones today. overlooked
once again :(

16. June 21.21

No. the number 8 and the heart were both from me =
yours always :)

16. June 22.15

Angry and horny sounds weird. But actually a rather
attractive mixture! but have 2 admit Im really down.

16. June 22.20

Is that last symbol a cunt? whew! now ur talking big boy!

16. June 22.30

Ill let u rip off my skirt and panties and take me from behind. abandon myself 2 u completely. let u dominate me and move me whatever way u want with ur hard hands. Ill just totally indulge in it! :) kisses and safe journey 2 Spain and c u in a weeks time. kisses baby.

. . .

25. June 20.16

Wow r u back already J?

25. June 20.31

Oh yesterday? so u only had 2 go for a short trip? musta picked that up wrong.

. . .

26. June 14.15

Busy? mental more like. the days have just flown by.

26. June 14.32

Ah yeah. Im sure we can catch up at some point. Lærke being very fkin difficult at the moment tho. so cant say precisely when.

. . .

27. June 12.26

I've a million and one things 2 get done b4 the summer break. so dont know if well get seein each other b4 me and Lærke head off on our holidays. Sry.

27. June 15.07

Like I said. Ive a million and one things on my plate.

27. June 15.10

Well well just have 2 wait until august 2 c each other wont we?

. . .

28. June 23.37

Jonah. hope ur OK. but thought I better let u know in fairness 2 u that something pretty drastic and crazy has happened here. Ill defo explain at some later point. but cant say any more about it right now . . .

. . .

29. June 13.26

Look I just cant say a thing about whats going on right now cuz not all the affected parties have been informed yet.

29. June 13.41

U just have 2 accept that theres someone I have 2 talk 2 bfore I can reveal anything 2 u. all I can say is that

reality has once again become stranger than fiction.
a crazy turn of events right out of the blue. ull get ur
explanation as soon Im able 2 give it.

29. June 14.06

Im not going 2 keep repeating myself Jonah. theres just
a few others who are b4 u in the queue.

29. June 14.30

Of course ull b told what its all about. we cant c each
other anymore. I admit its a bummer ur being informed
by text. but really thats ur fault cuz ur forcing me 2 do
it. and of course I want 2 explain. if ur interested in why
that is. but itll only b when Im ready and able 2 do it!

29. June 15.03

No. no. wrong Jonah. I actually dont owe u any
explanation whatsoever. as I said ur not the main priority
in this and right now Im only thinking about me and the
family Ive fucked up.

29. June 17.30

OK. But 4 a start u totally have 2 accept my explanation.
no ifs or buts. and then secondly Im assuming u will
keep ur trap totally shut about it. do u promise?

29. June 17.39

As Ive already said. I do NOT owe u any explanation
whatsoever. but yes I want 2 give u one – eventually. but
I wont tell u a thing Jonah if I cant trust u. cuz this is so

fkin top secret. only a very few people know about it and it really must not be leaked out. Im assuming u will never 4give me but Im sure I can live with that.

29. June 17.56
No Ive not deceived u any more than Ive deceived myself and my family. so were all equal.

29. June 18.18
OK. here goes. Ive been hit by lightning. Ive fallen in love with Petra. and she naturally has 2 explain things 2 her partner. now ex partner. so as u can imagine weve quite a few practical things 2 sort out. this of course will take a while. u more than anyone should understand that these things happen. and that they nearly always happen at the weirdest moments. I know its not particularly nice 4 most of those affected. but right now I have 2 put me first and get things sorted. of course we can c each other at some point if u think thats a gud idea. but as I say only when things r fully settled and theres loadz of things still 2 b organised.

29. June 18.35
Ah fuck J dont start all that. those horny messages I sent were b4 u went 2 Spain. and while u were gone I went on that weekend staff break 2 Berlin. I told u about it remember? it was in Berlin the whole thing exploded and there was absolutely nothing b4 that. so quit with all that crap about me being sly and taking u 4 a ride!

2

9. June 18.55

Me? cold and heartless? Jonah lets get this fkin straight. YOU were the one that started our "thing" and laid down the conditions. Ive never promised u anything watsoever. so dont dare fkin presume u have a say in my life. cuz its me not u that has 2 take care of certain people and I wont let u crush them or get near them. we both know the rules about relationships and both knew from the start what we were getting into. dont start crying about it now ffs.

29. June 19.10

Ur friends? ur friends? WTF does any of this have 2 do with ur friends? think very carefully b4 u do something u will regret. do u think ur the only 1 thats stressed about all this? well think again! Jesus H Christ what a fkin martyr!

29. June 19.22

Listen very very carefully Jonah. this has FUCK ALL 2 do with ANY of friends or family. now. ur going 2 keep ur fucking mouth shut about us. if u dont ull b sorry cuz I can destroy ur career if I have 2.

29. June 19.36

No its never occurred 2 me 2 mention "us" 2 anyone else. NEVER. it wasnt that kind of thing. sure it was gr8 fun and we got on well as u say but thats all dead + 4gotten as a dodo and theres no point going on about it. end of story.

JULY

1. July 09.21

Jonah. Im really sorry uve been readmitted 2 hospital. but u know how things r now and that I just cant be there 4 u in any shape or form. and anyway its not even a good idea. Im also up 2 my tits here with a million things. but look. no hard feelings. I really hope they look after u and get u better. and do by all means text me occasionally 2 tell me how things are going if u want. but ull understand that I wont be able 2 reply. life moves on.

. . .